PRAISE FOR KANSASTAN

"Halal fiction, blessed with an intensely stylized, lyrical syntax. The narrator's voice summons the faithful more clearly than a muezzin's call. *Kansastan* offers us the pure truth of divinity— or, closer to reality, a wildly intelligent caper."

Amitava Kumar
author of Immigrant, Montana

"Holy shit, we are definitely not in Kansas anymore. And Farooq Ahmed is like no novelist this world has seen. Brutally funny and disruptive, *Kansastan* is a work of alternative history that finally seems more true, more real, and more painfully strange and sad, than the world it replaces."

Ben Marcus
author of Notes from the Fog

"Imagine Kansas as a state with a grand mosque and a powerful Islamic tradition. Imagine a border war against the ruffian Missourians. A questionable savior. A group of zealous, devout Muslim fighters led by a man named Brown. That's the world of Farooq Ahmed's outstanding novel *Kansastan*. From the first line, Ahmed's extraordinary literary and political mind makes this book feel inevitable, moving, and American in every way. Prepare to be amazed."

Whitney Terrell
author of The Good Lieutenant

KANSASTAN

a novel by

Farooq Ahmed

7.13 Books
Brooklyn, NY

Printed and distributed by 7.13 Books. First paperback edition, first printing: Sept 2019

Cover design: Matthew Revert
Photo credit: Joanna Spilker

ISBN-13: 978-1-7328686-8-7

Library of Congress Control Number: 2019942226

For my cousin, Faisal.

Would that he had lived a shorter life.

"Your Lord revealed to the bees: Build your hives in mountains, trees and in what people build. These are signs for those who contemplate."

—Your Lord

"When I strike, the bees will begin to swarm, and I want you to help hive them."

—John Brown

THE SIX-LEGGED STEER

Let my clouds be cleared.

Exhale as you say it: *In the name of the Almighty, Gracious, and Merciful Lord.*

Three events in my life happened in seemingly quick succession that have led to my confinement in a chamber atop a minaret in eastern Kansas: The first was my arrival at the mosque that harbors this minaret. The second: the arrival of familial relations, an aunt and her son, from a far-off and to me indistinct land. And the third: the arrival of my love, Ms. A_____, from the same territory.

And here it is revealed if you choose to listen no further: Ms. A_____ is the mother of *my child*—not my cousin's child, not the Savior's child, as is widely and incorrectly assumed— but my child, *my son!*

The boy is the son of F_____! Not the son of Faisal!

F_____ the Redeemer! Not Faisal!

The Lord be praised!

It all began on a parched morning. At an age some might call tender, I huddled in the bed of a cattle cart. I was not a man then by our traditions, but I was old enough for the hand calluses and the like. And I was not alone. Heaped like wheat stalks, a dozen bodies crowded around me.

In the ways of our people, those who claimed the

descendants of Ibrahim's eldest son as their familials—Hajar's son, not Sarah's—the departed were bound in layer-over-layer of muslin. Blood stained the cloth in rust-colored blooms as if the casualties hadn't been cleansed, but they had: A biting odor, camphor, clouded the cart.

Men, women too, had been dispatched, murdered, posted through to the other side. Maybe there were children or just the meat of the once able-bodied. Nothing very uncommon.

Did I know how the dead populated the cart? I did not. Perhaps I alone had survived whatever calamity that claimed my brethren. Perhaps my parents shared their fate. I was not told. A feast on my knowledge, I should admit, would starve a meadow mouse.

The same muslin that covered the dead bound my own head, and my fingers found my scalp but felt no insult, no ghastly sutures sewed by an itinerant healer. But I was not then nor am I now addlebrained! The bandages jaundiced from sweat and stunk, but my mind was sweet.

Slender iron machinations encased both of my spindly legs. The devices pained me, but they were medicinal and forestalled my feet from curling inwards, rendering me fully lame. They had arrived in the hidebound suitcase on which I rested my head. The machinations of medicine to mend what the Almighty molded!

The cart rolled and pitched. We were not in a hurry. We were not being chased as in a children's game, but I could not guess to where we were going.

The astringent scent of my cadaverous companions was soon joined by another: that of sweet tobacco emanating from the drover, who with a staff, beat the steer that hauled us. The drover was a man scraped of flesh with a bucket hat crushed low across his eyes. If he was my Ibrahim, then I was his Hajar or Ismail. His service to the Lord: to abandon my person in this desolate country. And mine: to accept exile and resettlement in return for progeny who would rule over this land.

It was a fair barter, as are all the Lord's arrangements, for He is the Embodiment of Justice. But of course, I did not know this at the time.

The drover cried, "Hup hup," as we labored along. The old man removed his cap and uncovered a hairless dome and a pinched face, long and narrow, almost as if his mother had bedded a common squirrel! It provoked a laugh, but I suppressed crowing, because I was merciful.

Although I would see the man often in later years and would be partially responsible for his disfigurement, I realize now that I should have capitalized on my delight at the first time witnessing his comical visage. It deserved a mild howl. You cannot say that I have not learned to take advantage of the opportunities the great Lord presents. He offers only so many of them to believers, which is what we were. What I still am! The Lord be praised.

In any case, I did not even chuckle at this man, though I studied him hard. The words "Kansas Undertakers Department" were scrawled across the back of his overalls, and beneath this inscription palsied hands, perhaps the same ones that had not sutured my head, had stitched an outline of our State. Poor craftsmanship exaggerated our uncomplicated borders. The slogan beneath read *ad Astra per Aspera* in a flaxen thread, which every schoolchild knew to mean: *to the stars with adversity*. Our State's motto for the moment. It provided little comfort.

I called out to the old man respectfully, because I was respectful, "Sir. Sir," but he did not hear me. Perhaps the seething wind ate my words. A cart wheel slammed into a rut and thrust me into the air. My sole possession, the suitcase, broke my fall and sprung open. It revealed nothing, and I snapped it shut. The mummies shuddered. My head throbbed, and I wished dearly for a bedroll on which to lay it. But I had only corpses for comfort. If I had been launched clear of the tailgate, it would have been the first of my failed escapes.

I remember the sky broke above us—a bomb bleaching the bleached vault—and I flattened myself against the cart.

Spit upon saying their names: Savages. Terrorists. Irregulars. Pukes. Missourians. Vile, long-haired wrecks who haunted the cow paths that crosscut our State and executed sudden torments on the passersby. Their primitive customs foreswore the taking of prisoners, so their violence could not be undone, only revenged. Almost certainly my travelling companions were the ruins of their handiwork. Our varied and splendid lives cut short by our erstwhile neighbors to the east.

The drover seemed immune to the bellicosity and clucked to his skittish beast. Neither did a thing to quicken our pace. If we were being pursued, we would be overcome, and two more would join the congregants in the back of the cart. Such was the sorrowful mathematics of warfare. And although I remain poor at ciphering, I could sum this much.

In this manner, wedged against the dead, I peered through the cattle cart's splintered gates for a tour of our State. We cut across fields and interminable greenswards that lured our malnourished steer with their deliciousness. We broke across scrub and stubble and the thistle that towered over the grasses like watchmen. We weaved around fields of tall grasses, which undulated like the mane of a bobcat in wintertime but were just hell to traverse. When I glimpsed a thicket, it seemed to spring from my imagination as an oasis. A vestige from a resolute and less-domesticated era.

But there was no water until the drover led us through a wide pass into a valley sprinkled with wildflowers. It was a sight. Jackrabbits hammered at each other, then scurried away at the approach of our noise. Their droppings perfumed the field. You would have thought the place as fertile as Gethsemane!

It was not hard to see how faith took hold here, even if my cousin and his mother manufactured the miracles—of this I was certain! With all that bloody border-crossing, abundance was not in abundance. In the stories we were told, the ones I overheard from my distinguished post at the rear of our prayer hall or in our begrimed coffeehouse—which was the home to my worm-lipped love, the mother of *my child*, not my cousin's, but *my child*—in those old stories, illustrious men of the desert enacted the divine under distant and cloudless skies. At the behest of the Lord Seated Comfortably in His Throne in Heaven.

That morning, I witnessed that our land is a cousin to that ancient, miracle-strewn terrain: Despite its occasional verdancy, both shared broad expanses of uninterrupted country and a vast sky, often somber and unmarred by clouds. The monotony was broken by storms and flying pestilence, but if you were looking for guidance and cleaved fastly to scripture then you would find our land fertile for salvation.

We halted only once on that journey that delivered me to the mosque in which I have resided save for the brief and harrowing period after the regrettable incidents at my cousin's funeral. (But I will not speak of them now!)

The squirrel-faced drover navigated like he was familiar with the place, and we reached a creek that cut through the valley. We stopped to water ourselves and fulfill our obligations to the Lord, but the lout made a mockery of these honest tasks.

The old man snuffed a smoke, dropped from his stoop above the beast and adjusted himself as he unharnessed the animal. A pair of withered legs grew from the steer's neck as if another calf had tried and failed to escape from the same hide. Someone had been tender to this beast: Both of its unneeded limbs had been shod, though I did not know why one would lavish iron on hooves that did not call for them. Why such fancy in a time of privation and need? It suited no one.

The steer wore a languid expression as it struggled against the drover who guided it by these shod appendages to brook. What a specimen it was.

I slid to the open end of the cart and took care to not molest the fallen. As I tumbled to the ground in my unpoetic way, a strap from my leg brace snagged the muslin shroud of one of our departed and revealed flaked lips and rusted nubs of teeth. I scoured the face of this man for an affirmation of familial physiognomy. I found none. In this matter, not remembering fully what my own face looked like was also not a help.

"To Him shall we return," I mumbled an old prayer and readjusted the fabric, relieved that neither the drover nor the steer was vigilant of my transgression.

I struggled against the switchgrass—a conspiracy of nature!—until finally I arrived downstream of the beast and its master who knelt at the stream as if in prayer. Cupping my hands, I filled and drained and filled them again with the cool wash before I raised them to my lips.

The drover scooped creek water into the bucket of his cap and then launched it at the steer in a long billowy sheet. The wash ricocheted off the animal and spittled onto me, and I felt anointed against the heat. The man removed his boots and threadbare socks and again filled his hat to proceed with ablutions. The steer dipped in its plump tongue, which dangled from its slow mouth like overripe fruit. I longed for a blade to liberate that fruit, to satiate my hunger. The Lord be praised.

Although I was not inclined—I have never understood this custom of our people, the need for constant cleansing as if they soil themselves with great ease and frequency—I bathed as well and spilled the rinse across my person, careful to not flood my bindings. I was grateful for the cool.

Once I ungrimed myself, I went in for a sip. I mimicked the beast and lapped up the wash, which now tasted of brine. I savored it on my tongue, when I heard the old man shatter with laughter. I gulped down the brackish water and saw the man collapse in the field, curled like a submitting hound. He wheezed out a fresh sound like a boy being strangled.

It seemed as if as I sipped, the drover had micturated in the stream! Pissed in it as I drank! To laugh at the expense of an orphaned boy! And this from a believer! I dove into the creek to drown my mouth. The current nearly swept the wrapping off my head. Adversity indeed!

I dried myself as I could and scowled at the steer who remained unmoved by my situation. Rage clotted my throat. I wanted to waste the old man with a mouth war. Skin and roast him on a spit like a squirrel in the evening.

The drover recovered from his spasms and then proceeded—as if no foul had occurred!—to spot the sun, regarding our compass for prayer. The old man folded his arms across a rangy chest and rasped out entreaties to the Lord.

I thought about how vulnerable the Mahometan was when in the act of prayer. How a supplicating head seemed fit for the executioner's blade. Maybe we all awaited that axe, and our submission merely delayed it?

Yet, I could not....

The man's choked laughter had quieted me. It was as if his exertions had meted out a portion of the drover's life. It seemed a fair and in fact a hallowed trade: the hastening of his demise in exchange for my humiliation. The Lord be praised.

(I took comfort in this notion but in time would learn that it was misguided—a product of a desperate imagination that craved a divine and brutal justice. I would learn, rather, that the Great Will of the Almighty needed hands through which to strike, and that even the categorically lame, such as myself, could discharge the Lord's honorable work. Was it not said that: *Chosen in Heaven, Holy Work must still be created by man?*)

It was at times like this, though, that I missed having a benevolent patriarch in my life. Perhaps a father. Perhaps if I had, I would not be trapped in a crumbling tower while my martyred cousin's minions march merrily against the Missourians. With the minaret I began, and with it I shall end!

A curtain has been drawn over those times—times when I may have held the thick wrists of a father as he sailed my frailty through an arc in the evening sky. Father: Would that I had a face to put that kind word to.

Our prayers concluded, I asked the drover where we were going. His tongue rested in his mouth as if his words would nourish me. As if they would nourish me and starve him in the process. Would that they would.

But there was no time to think of it. He twisted another smoke then directed his response, a firm, "Hup hup," to the snub-horn. With mild hardship, I returned to the charnel in the back, and the cart lurched forward.

I persevered. This is, after all, a story of my perseverance in the face of familial, sectarian, and international persecution—in that order.

Above us hovered the fat form of a warship blimp. A golden braid trailed from it like the tail of a kite. Not Missourians. I pointed at the dirigible and asked squirrel-face if he saw it. He glanced upwards, any response a victory of a sort, then scowled. His disgust was more terrifying than his amusement, and he returned to his mute ways.

I rested my bandaged head on my valise. Inured to the bucking of the cart, I drifted off, watching the flame that trailed the blimp.

A blast—Missourians!—roused me. Their bombs infallible at waking even a dwale-drunk Jay-hawker.

I searched the skies for that blimp. Where was it?

Gone.

(I would think about that blimp often enough to believe that I could summon it.)

The sun had outrun us too. It roosted ahead like a blazing buzzard. It reminded me of a line from scripture: *Enjoy yourselves, for your destination is the Fire*. It should be said that only on a rare occasion did the Good Book console rather than torment me. This was not one of those occasions.

But there was good news that morning! (Or so I thought). The horizon birthed the tall and curious form of a single, overgrown birch tree. On a cottonwood-bedeviled prairie, it was an unusual but not an unfamiliar site. It required husbandry. Only the cedar was native here. I propped myself atop an unsteady pyramid of corpses to see it better, but the steer's expendable hooves obstructed the view.

As we lurched forward, the humdrum hocus-pocus of heat-blasted vision corrected the birch, which was not a tree but rather a steeple severed from its chapel. Closer still, it emerged again as a minaret—a pale and knotted finger raised high on a fist of earth. As I had not known that smoldering morning that this was my destination, so I could not have predicted that this slender form would be my home and my penitentiary—the place where I now rest my unbandaged head, and the place in which I will never find rest.

And if he had known it, the drover confessed this to me no more than he did his name.

A minaret on the plains was still an unusual site. But in this post-Republic era, with brother against brother and sister reloading rifles, more of them had appeared. Minarets colonized disremembered steeples and other failed ziggurats—dismantled orthodoxies swapped for other, more vigorous and fully bearded ones.

We held this as a truth: One did not withstand mischief-makers by relying on frail, cheek-turning deities. The steadfast silhouettes of minarets came to testify that despite the nastiness that emanated from our east, a righteous Hand guided us on the plains. Our Lord suffered no occupiers without retribution and the angelic clang of retribution's counterplay. For the Lord is the Reckoning One.

No minaret stood to use without a mosque, and such a structure lurked nearby. From our distance, it too glimmered, and I shaded my face with a curl of muslin to better spy. A crescent moon of bronze, or if I may be fanciful—of gold—capped a moss-green dome. The mosque's windows were so plentiful one might have thought sheet glass was as common as chalk. The windows mirrored the fractured clouds to make the sanctuary seem celestial. One would be unashamed to call such a place home, and you might imagine how excited I grew as we neared.

This elation, I have learned, was the product of a Fool's Faith. And if I was a fool, then you will remember that Ismail was called a wild-ass of a man.

As nothing else inhabited this lonely corner of our Country, I presumed that we were to deposit our sorry cargo and slumber at this house of worship. I thought that perhaps the soles of our feet would be cleansed by a reverent custodian, and we would be fed a wheat porridge.

But the trail spooled relentlessly before us, and to relieve the tedium I harvested grasses from the fastenings of my leg braces and surrendered them from the tail of the cart as if they were breadcrumbs. The clovers I secreted in the lap of my tunic until I collected a ransomable amount, then weaved them into the cloth band around my head. Would that I had a true crown. The Lord be praised.

As finally we approached, I noticed a rubble wall that fashioned the edge of the mosque compound. The rocks were rounded like weathered headstones as if to serve as a warning to any who entered that the afterlife awaited. This wall, if you could call it that, terminated at a forest that cozied up to the minaret.

A herd of goats, tassels dangling from their throats, manicured the brambles. The pack brought with them a rude smell and dodged beneath our cart. A game for them that I thought would for us surely end in sustenance. I held my breath. Even the departed would have held theirs too. Why had the Creator fashioned a world so foul? Was it to hasten us to His light?

The drover spat on a finger and with it quenched his tobacco. Then, he jerked on the reins and leveraged his decrepitude against the steer. We halted at a break in the stone wall from which a flyspecked path forked to the mosque's arched entryways. I took this to be the approved entrance to the compound, though even an infirm, not-quite-man such as me could have at any point scaled the barrier. I was not strong, but I was clever.

The mute drover landed his staff on the meat of my shoulder and forced me off the corpses into the dust. Above us, the sky roared again, and I dropped to the trail bed. Foam-mouthed vermin! I cursed. Sarah-loving sons of Quantrill! I spat on the trail.

The drover discerned that the blast was from a nearby chalk-mining concern—they were constantly blasting our land for the precious mineral—and he choked out a laugh, bemused by my oaths as if I was the prize japer at the State Fair. For a moment, his rodent face seized, and I thought I would witness his sudden expiration. Which would have pleased me to no end.

The menace passed, and I massaged the spot of the old man's assault—his second of the day on my infirm person!

The drover cried out to the animal and made no attempt to unload the dead. Just as it seemed he might incinerate himself and his regretful cargo in the fireball of the sun that engulfed the horizon, he hooked the cart in a lazy half-circle. I shaded my eyes, and he tossed my suitcase so that it landed alongside me in the dust. It again sprung open and exposed my scarcity of secrets. I snapped it shut.

The six-legged steer returned along the path from whence we'd come. Would that I had found the strength to steal that old man's staff, pry him from his seat, and joyride that steer into a more hospitable land. Beautiful Bountiful Colorado!

Instead, I was welcomed to the mosque by those rank goats.

The herd encircled me in their ungeometric way and worked the bristles of their tongues into my leg braces. I felt like I was being eaten alive by tiny wet mouths and was left encrusted in ropes of their saliva. The beasts scoured the metal buckles until they shone. So, it was these reverent custodians, I thought, who would offer me cleansing.

The trash-eaters gnawed at the straps. My harnesses slackened, and I swung my case at them. Although armed, I was harmless, but the goats scattered, nonetheless. Save for one, who continued to work his wet tongue between my toes. Industrious beast!

I could not help but think that until I learned to draw a red line across their throats with a knife consecrated for such purposes, I had lost standing among the creatures that inhabited the world, be it man or others: goats, steers.

I looked above me. Where else would you look? Still no blimp. The moon found its high station, but sunlight flooded us as if to prevent the coming of evening. I discerned from this celestial communion that the day still held a pair of prayers—prayers that promised the arrival of worshippers. I refastened my leg braces and scraped toward the sanctuary.

Up close, the mosque's grandeur was unmasked as decrepitude. It reminded me of a sad and abused town hall. Canyons broke across the turban of a dome. Dark birds casually vandalized it with their impolite offerings. The once-glorious windows, which stood at the height of our tallest men and the length of our most exquisite oxen, reflected only the animals that tended the grounds. The glass was streaked with mud and peppered with copper pellets. The crescent hung askew and threatened to crash down on worshippers, when any would appear.

Soot ringed the minaret. It was as if after previous service as a smokestack, it had been slathered in whitewash and left to season in rough weather.

The mosque and the minaret also sat at a queer angle to each other, as though they had congressed reluctantly. And if geometry can be said to affect personal relations, then surely the unease between my cousin—who went to the Garden of Immortality as Commander of the Faithful—and myself, who has yet to go to his grave, can be explained by this inadequate architecture and our habitations within.

On the other side from the minaret, against the mosque's opposite flank, a pair of tin and wood sheds deteriorated in the heat—an outhouse and slaughterhouse I suspected. A grave-yard and a cart stacked with corpses, I thought, was all that was needed to complete this grim scene. I slapped at a gnat and kicked up dust. Chirrs chirped.

As I approached the holy place, one mottled fellow escaped the herd and trotted alongside me. The nubs of the fiend's horns threatened to impale my delicate person. So agitated, I swung an appendage at him.

The beast squirted between my legs, and suddenly I found myself astride it as it bucked forward. My feet dragged in the gravel, and away we rode.

In this manner—clutching an empty leather case, my leg braces glistening with goat slather, my head swathed in a crown of muslin and clover, and riding a goat that I would slaughter in a year's time—I entered the Great Mosque of the Holy State of Kansas.

And like his own entrance: No flowers were strewn or drums beaten. In fact, there seemed to be no soul to guide us.

A MOSQUE

What is a mosque?
A place for worship, certainly. That much we all know.

Is it a place for reflection?
Only when performed silently.

Is it a site for the miraculous, the unexplained?
So the Brothers, my aunt, and the imam would have you believe.

Could it be a home?
Yes, of a sort.

Is it suitable for adolescents to inhabit?
No one should have the sanctity of their accommodations overrun multiple times a day by the worshipful—so says my experience.

Can it be used as a town hall? A site from which religious and political directives are issued?
The Lord be praised!

Can it serve as a military installation?
Should the need arise, when evildoers may be bested with
divine assistance.

*May it find use as an encampment for displaced persons, expatriates,
escapees, emigrants, Delegates and the like?*
No house of worship should be used for such a purpose—
that is what reason tells us! But herein lays a conundrum! If it
weren't for this purpose, I should not have encountered the
mother of my son.

THE FIELD OF MEAT

Atop the goat of my deliverance, I galloped to the mosque's arched stone entryways. We clattered past the minaret, which the sun lit like a fiery beacon fallen from Heaven even as grime crusted its façade. Ravens perched atop the mosque and eyed me in their contrary way. I expected them to rouse and attack as if to say, "to hell with you, invader."

I dismounted and walloped the kid's flank. He slurped my hand—dirty beast!—but heeled to my side as if I were guilty of his domestication. I did not argue with the instant kinship I felt. Then, he scurried away between the mosque and the minaret as if to spite me.

I hobbled over to investigate the suspect treasures of the mosque. My feet filthy, hunger tore at me, and the damned chirrs chirred.

I pressed myself into the warmth of the windows. Exquisite, desolate, nothing about the place suggested that it had sustained anything, neither life nor faith. A thing built, blessed, and then forgotten. For a moment, I feared I had been left by the drover to fend for myself—a final insult.

But what should one do when one arrives uninvited to a house of worship? This, I did not know.

What did Hajar do when Ibrahim abandoned her and Ismail in the desert? She nearly died of thirst, that's what.

I stepped back to inspect my reflection. My initiation into our flock and with it my official passage from boy- to man-hood would happen years later, but down edged onto my cheeks as no blade had graced my face. I was near Ismail's age when Sarah begat Ishaq, I also liked to think.

And I was not unhandsome for a cripple child! Were my clothes tattered? Yes, but they could be mended. Was my head injured? If so, it would heal. Did I lean precipitously to the right? No, although I did seem to flatter that side. Could my cheeks have used fattening? Certainly, but I was not alone in courting this defect. My eyes and nose were as they should have been: prominent, defiant, unbloodied. Ordained for a great purpose!

In truth, my countenance approached that of those noble and fearsome Fanatics who buried empires. If one overlooked the clatter of my stride.

Through the glass and beyond my pale reflection, light spilled into the assembly hall. A bird fluttered between the pillars. It rose in a misguided belief that freedom could be purchased through the cracks in the dome. Prayer rugs were stacked along a wall. Several chambers sprouted from the main hall and stairs led downwards. But inside was a place into which I did not yet venture.

The minaret captured my attention. If habitations and their inhabitants can be said to have an affinity that stretches beyond this world, then surely, I felt drawn to it. A red slat door like one to a cellar or stable sealed it shut, and a bolt secured it from the outside. I escalated a slight ledge to reach this port, which exhaled an earthy smell like something dug up.

As I had suspected, the minaret was a sham. A thing built for another purpose, carted here to impress the impressionable. Instead of a monument to the Lord, it was brick and mortar slathered in lime. Brick could not ape stone, this much I knew. The knowledge filled me with an occult sense of pride, even an arrogance.

The kid goat circled behind the mosque, and I followed in my clumsy-footed way. The sanctuary stood on high ground above a field that stretched behind, and my companion and I stumbled down the slight slope to discover a maze of blistered wood and stone so haphazardly strewn as to seem hieroglyphic. Whatever had been civilizing this place in the pre-mosque time, a charred shrine was all that remained.

I made my way to the ruin, eager to uncover any odd, unkempt fortunes abandoned by the previous inhabitants. The burdensome scent of roasting goat made its way to me, but my hunger was for a moment extinguished by adventure. Would that all our appetites could so easily be satiated.

That is when I encountered him. A man who had many names. My infrequent father: Imam Bahira.

The imam, our so-called spiritual leader, had the stately proportions of an ordinary man living in a blighted world. He wore, as I did, a cream-colored tunic that hugged his bloated form, but his was less yellowed. He had pinned a sunflower to it, keeping with the fashion of our times, which, let it be said, compelled you to profess your faith, your affiliation, lest you be mistook and erroneously and unceremoniously executed. Also like me, the imam was not shod.

But apart from his stature, what was truly marvelous was his face. It wore a fearsome cloak of hair: The upper lip was shorn, but the cheeks, jaw, and chin full-bristled. This beard was vital, menacing, the hue of a shriveled riverbed when shocked with spring water. This wooly face loomed below a white knit cap.

The imam ambled through the wreckage. He moved with a stoop, as though he conversed with an unseen diminutive. With the ease of a celebrated whittler, he slivered a hunk of meat. Rain came by way of the scraps. Fluttering around him were dozens of blackbirds that snatched up his offerings in their ungallant way and tossed the scraps down their gullets.

I insinuated myself against the back of the mosque as if I could dissolve into it. Unaware of my slight presence, the imam continued seeding the field with this flesh as a farmer might sow grain. I once again could not fathom the purpose of such a wasteful act in these sun-beaten times.

Compelled by hunger, I dared to scavenge those scraps for myself and toss them down my own ravenous gullet, if a tender-foot can be said to have one. I was not addlebrained, but I was also not a scholar. Although I had no chance to not be seen by this giant, I scraped forward and soon lay crouched at the edge of the meat-laden field and harvested morsels with crows.

A vigilant hawk swooped from an unseen perch and crashed into the imam. It clawed at the sleeve of his tunic, and the oily flock scattered at the war bird's arrival.

The man withstood the hawk's onslaught and seduced the creature atop his forearm with a scrap of goat. The knife drooped from his grasp as the talons scored his flesh, and I was close enough that if I had been a different sort of fiend, I could have snatched the blade and caused no small harm to either monster or man. But as I have mentioned I was respectful.

Then the imam did a thing I had never seen: He whispered to the bird, and it retreated, a sliver hanging from its mouth as it flew away.

At the sight of this conversation, half-formed words stumbled from my lips and revealed my stupid position. The imam swung around to find me crouching behind him, his eyebrows tornado-swept, conferring a fury to his face that I thought was certain to break upon me in that moment. A necklace of prayer beads, heavy as stone, thumped against his barrel chest with such resonance that you'd have thought the preacher hollow rather than filled with rich liquids. That the hawk left no incisions on his flesh, I was in disbelief.

If the imam was surprised to encounter me—my bandaged head sprouting clovers, tufts of black hair like the leaves of a bitter dandelion, soiled gown reeking of sweat and goat love, and gangly legs encased in iron, crouched like an animal devouring the scraps he had cast aside—he did not betray it. He greeted me instead in an ancient manner, wishing me peace.

His voice, small and reedy for his stature, then asked, "Boy? Boy, can you stand?" It occurs to me in hindsight that this question was simply the fruit of his dull expectations for my person. Someone, perhaps that nasty drover, had likely informed the imam of my arrival and abject condition.

Before rising, I filched up a handful of scraps and crammed them into my mouth. On my feet, I stood to the height of the imam's chest, which in these foreshortened times felt like an accomplishment. He unwrapped my head like a Festival present, the clovers sprinkling down, then palpated my skull as if I were a roadside apple seller's prized harvest. He scoured my scalp, perhaps searching for cracks or vermin and yanked at my ears among other affronts.

Then in a motion that had, I assume, no precedent and certainly no antecedent, he mashed his cheek to mine first on one side and then the other and battered me about as if I were a small ship and he a storm at sea. Up close, his beard smelled of tart eucalyptus, and goat fat.

"The Lord is great for sending me a child. You are the boy, no?" he asked. I, unsure of what else he might expect me to be, answered affirmatively. The goat on which I rode, appeared then from a foray deep into the charred village and scrounged bits of meat. The imam tossed my head wrap to the little trash-eater.

I swept an appendage over the rubble and asked, "What is this place?" unsure that my words would register after their earlier and regular disregard by the drover.

The imam unfurled the expected response: "What else? Terrorists!" and then he spat on the ground. His beard flashed crimson, and I thought it a grand affectation.

The mosque, he seemed to imply, stood on the grounds of a previous institution that had been found wanting by Missourian Bushwhackers, and so they set upon it with torches. As was their wont.

Then he asked me: "May I? Would you, permit me to inspect your cloak?"

"My tunic?" I bleated.

He spun my indelicate form about and seemed to audit my neck, back, and shoulders for marks or blemishes, to what ends, I could not guess. Was I the one sprouting hooves from the meat of my neck?

After having submitted to this curious interrogation, I pulled away.

"Come," the goliath said, "let us take you to your home," and the imam bounded to the mosque. I struggled in pursuit as he strode to a rear, basement door that, like the entryway to the minaret, seemed repurposed from a stable.

Thus, it was that my first entrance into the sanctuary was not through the regal stone archways, but instead via this inglorious passage. That chance had lowered the circumstances of my arrival in this holy place to no better than that of a graceless miner was an insult I would later rectify. The goat attempted to follow us into the mosque and received a swift foot to the flank. As I have learned, ungulates are particularly unwelcome in houses of worship.

Once inside, I could see to where the stairs had descended. Haze filtered from the mosque's top level to this cavernous cellar, which reeked of gunpowder. The unfinished floors felt chicken-scratched to my bare feet. I thought I heard a bat squawk and saw a tabby slink down a hallway, but it might have been another large vermin.

The preacher led us to the stairs, instruments that have bedeviled me all my short and wondrous life. I struggled as he bounded up—a feat that seemed to mock my own reduced abilities. The imam glanced back, "They couldn't send a whole boy?" he asked and laughed in short, galumphing bursts. It made me long for the drover's silent malice.

I had finally ascended into the mosque's hall, when I spied the imam already outside. I slid across the tile as the trapped sparrow attempted to escape. It fluttered and failed and fluttered and failed again. What could I do to assist its departure? The problem vexed me, but no ready solution appeared: I could neither snare the bird nor enlargen a crack.

Do they not see the birds above them? Nothing upholds them except for the Lord, I thought.

A week later, I would encounter the warm, fluttering carcass of this bird and cook it on a spit in the ruins of the mosque's backyard. Defeathering, however, was not a task with which I have had much familiarity or luck!

As I exited the mosque, the imam opened the minaret's stable door. "Here you are son," he bellowed, employing an undeserved moniker. "Your room, top. Rest. Come down for prayers. Then, then we will begin your work." Words spoken as if commanded from on High. Would that a tenderfoot could slay a giant.

He swatted me across the shoulders, and because I was dutiful, I scraped into the tower. Shattered bottles littered the vestibule. What was this place, I thought, but a haven for secret drunkards or others who make plots at night? A smile formed on my cowed and nearly hairless face. I swept the detritus out with my suitcase—it was my first custodial act as a resident and professional. The preacher shut the stable door behind me. Vermin squealed.

Even as sunlight speared through arrowslits, the inside of the minaret like the subterranean floor of the mosque felt damp. The scent of skunk permeated the tower, and a winding stone staircase confronted me. Suitcase in hand, I began my wavering ascent and showered sparks when the iron of my leg braces struck the stone. Would that the hard matter revered the flame like straw does.

I peered through the slits to spy on the glass-faced mosque, the creeping forest, and the field where I spotted my goat. I slid a slender arm through a gap and waved. Where had his herd gone? I did not know. The imam I also could not see. I counted the stairs as I ascended, and including the ledge at the foot of the minaret, I reached 101 by the time I arrived at a gunmetal slab that sealed what I supposed were my chambers.

I set my case by a lantern and oil tin left by the previous inhabitant. But the purpose for this elevated room escaped my industrious mind. Perhaps a silver-tongued bilal had dwelled here, and I would be groomed as his replacement! I cleared my throat and warbled out the call to prayer. I required training.

I drove my weight against the door, which squealed but would not give. Because I was clever, I slathered the castings with oil, and then with a lurch, open it slid! I would have yelped in delight except that with an ungainly leg I had propelled my case down the stairs. I descended and then re-ascended into a circular room atop the minaret, winded, soaked, but no longer hungry. A true triumph! May the Lord be praised!

This chamber atop the minaret became my home for much too long. (Except for a brief absence, which I should explain was not by choice, but one thrust upon me by hideous circumstance.) In time, I would whitewash the walls, standing on a stack of Holy Books before being felled by a kick to the flank by a father who had to crouch his way up to reach me on account of his massive frame.

But when I first entered, I recall the wind that chattered through the slab window, and against the opposite wall, a lumpy figure slept beneath a white shroud. I hobbled over, casting my shadow upon the slumbering form, and cleared my throat, *ashem ashem*. I stomped my iron feet. When finally I screwed the courage to lift the sheet, I found not a soul, but a straw mat, which when shook birthed stillborn mice. My suitcase fell to the floor, and I onto the mat.

At a late hour, I rose to congregants braying and mewling in the world beneath my perch. The wild melody of crickets skipped into my chambers, and moonlight flooded in as the Lord of the day had given way to the Lord of the night. For who can forget that the Lord loves a perfect symmetry. (And this symmetry executed on tormentors and infidels!)

I shook the straw from my hair, unfastened the bindings on my leg braces, and placed them inside the case. Liberated from their manufactured tyranny, I strummed my pigeon toes on the straw.

A series of shots popped off.

Not our industrious miners, but the craven chatter of unbelievers—Missourians!

Bedlam exploded below me.

I ignored the imam's earlier request and instead wriggled for defense beneath the straw mattress, comforted by the noble howl of prairie wolves and the timid light of firebugs.

When morning pierced through my window, on yearling's legs I stepped unbraced to explore the view. Forest creatures foraged in the branches, which shook in flurries. In the distance beyond the charred field behind the mosque, twin ribbons, one a burnt-earth color and the other a mud grey, cut across our land: cowpath and caravan trail. I followed them with the 'V' of my fingers until they escaped into the scalloped hills. A beautiful Country, I thought. This is a beautiful Country.

I rushed to discover what my new home offered and reached nearly halfway down the tower when I felt unbuttressed. In my haste, I had forgotten my leg braces.

Perhaps cousin, for liberating me from their tyranny, you *should* be thanked!

When I re-descended, I encountered a band of merchants that had transformed the plot in front of the mosque into a bazaar. It was the Prophet's day, Friday, and the reason for the screaming festivities: The weekly sermon drew its patrons.

Where I had conferenced with goats a day before, grocers performed buffooneries to amuse scampering, wet-mouthed children. Makeshift stalls had been erected, and corn and grains stacked and stored. Carts and coaches and colts and milking cows found themselves tethered to posts. A queue of citizens writhed by the outhouses, while an untended cauldron of chicory coffee infused the rowdy proceedings with a bitter warmth. If there was an order here, it was not a divine one.

I discovered the squirrel-faced drover among the rabble. One of his steer's superfluous legs had been liberated. A bandaged stump remained. The drover too was transformed—into a creature of water. The word "Undertakers" on the patch on his overalls had been replaced so that it read: "Kansas Water Department." The hacked outline of our State remained in its sad station.

From where the mummies had slumbered in the bed of his cart, the drover rolled sloshing barrels down a clapboard ramp. He courted his own congregation as the cotton-mouthed trailed him—the ecstasy on their faces evident as if he was the only clergyman in this parish.

Prior to the arrival of my relations, water was scarce in our State. Missourians—spit after saying it—staunched our harvesting vessels, particularly at the Kawsmouth where a convergence of rivers provided both a favorable harvesting station as well as an angling one.

But the drover was not one to beatify, of that I was certain. And while the old man wrangled an unruly barrel, I rewarded myself his tobacco from the perch of the cart.

Just then, a crowd burst from the mosque: the men of the plains and their women. Their faces were stained, creased, and cured like cowhide leather. The slight women draped themselves in scarves and bonnets, wisps of the selves these women would become. These citizens smelled of grease and hay. Of dust and chalk and sour yeast. Miners mingled with millworkers, savoring a break from the blasting and milling. The metropolitan men clamored into awaiting coaches, their steeds groomed and brushed, looking more elegant than many women I have seen. My ashen-faced love, Ms. A_____, excluded of course.

Although I had just arrived at the mosque, I envied these Kansans with their freedom to leave, with staircase-free homes where brethren may have embraced them and slapped hot oatcakes into their palms.

Fresh pocks marred the mosque's windows: Missourians! I excavated a copper pellet and slid it into my pocket.

I proceeded inside the dizzying hall where the tile was blanketed in prayer rugs. Into the rugs were stitched the form of the black square house to which we, like our remarkable forbearers, sent our daily entreaties to the Lord. The small black house that hived our prayers. Ibrahim's house. Ismail's house.

We prayed to a square, and soon our land, our Great State, will be a rectangle! The Lord loves a perfect symmetry for He is both the Maintainer of Life and Inflictor of Death. The Extender and the Reducer.

What I found in the prayer hall was men in soiled denim but with gleaming faces. They hunkered around the imam and listened transfixed as if he were a notable bard, which in these parts may have been an accurate rendering. I overheard their gripes: the fresh holes in the mosque; the paltry yields of their fields; the godless menace from the east.

"Ossawatomie, Marais des Cygnes, Wakarusa! All overrun!"

"Did you hear," one partisan snarled, "ruffians have been spotted in our forest!"

Missourians spooking our woods! The thought trembled me. Sometimes, I have learned, to gain knowledge is to court dread. And who needs that? The Lord be praised.

As I approached the group, in unison they mumbled about the greatness of the Lord and then dispersed as if they were awaiting my loathsome arrival. Was my presence such an affront to their sensibilities? Would that it was.

Dressed in a fine set of garments, the imam gestured for me to follow him. He led us to his chamber, which in comparison with my accommodations could have been those of the Grand Mufti of our State! He had a bedroll and a burnished desk of such heft that it could serve as a rampart should we ever be invaded like those trembling followers of Ishaq. On a wall, the piebald hide of a once-hooved beast splayed out. I would have liked to have been present for the harvest of its flesh.

The preacher slumped in his throne and popped the bristled end of a chewing stick into his mouth. He gnawed on it as he spoke, and with one bloated hand fingered his prayer beads as if the stones were an abacus. A licorice scent was on his breath—the flavor enchanting.

"You see," he leaned into me as he began, "you see we are here—we are here to purify this space." "We are here," he continued, measured, "to make it suitable for the Lord. And for man—to purify it for the Lord and for the men. For who knows how long we, the men, have to inhabit it? This world? This place? Our land?" His hands did things to indicate the presence of large spaces. And while the implications of his philosophy were not lost on me, I wondered how his stammering delivery could entrance even the most dimwitted of congregants!

"Even kings," he rambled, "those kings of the Holy House, the Square—you know the Square? The Cube?" With two fingers, he danced the simple form in the weather between us. "Yes, you know the Cube!" and his fist struck the desk. "Those kings are merely keepers. They are, in fact, the proudest custodians!" He said this to me as if I hadn't been schooled, and at that moment I could not recall if I had been.

The stick fell from his mouth onto the desktop and trailed spittle, which he mopped with the sleeve of his clerical tunic.

"Today, we shall begin by straightening up after the prayer." He droned on: "Stock the rugs. Sweep the floors. Burn the refuse. Martyr the goats. These are tasks you must do. The water, it has arrived? It has!" he bellowed, and his beard sparkled like a sunshower. "Refill the cistern—the cistern, it is below. Then you will return to me for I shall instruct you, son."

That word: son. It had an ineffable hold on me, like the stony grip of an angel on a nightly visitation. Oh, how the mighty enslave the meek with endearments!

Vanquished by that improper appellation, I slunk out of the imam's chambers and made my halting way to the cellar floor of the sanctuary. I recovered the instruments of my vocation from an untamed repository and then commenced the innumerable tasks I had been instructed to perform under the proscription that such labor was goodly if not Godly.

In truth, the tasks took less time to accomplish than I might have wagered, were we the wagering sort. The most arduous was refilling the cistern with those barrels carted here by the drover. As they sloshed about, I wondered how he could molest me even though I was no longer under his care. Devious employer!

As I have said, I was clever, so I knew to implement a slow-moving scheme and up-play my disabilities while executing these miserable tasks: I allowed the barrels to slip from my grasp as I uncarted them, and they careened into worshippers. When I swept, I waited until a father carted his napping child past me, and then my broom clattered to the tile. Oh, the shrieks I elicited! While ascending and descending stairs, I wailed like those startled babes but shrugged off assistance as if any touch would further injure me. On prayer rugs, I stumbled, and I clanked atop them so that they safekept my fracturable frame.

Over time, I became adept at this charlatanry. As I finished my chores from one prayer, another would begin so that I unfurled the rugs that I had only just finished stacking! Surely this was a victory. The Lord be praised!

When he was out of sight, I found a gratifying way to mimic the drover and began rolling smokes of my own. My first attempts were clumsy, and I choked through the mangled results. But soon, I discovered a rhythm and was glad that my ministrations at the mosque afforded me time to cultivate such an uplifting custom. Why there were not more in this world who partook I did not know, but it was a pleasurable activity.

It should be said, though, that my trickery was itself tiring. By the time the last devotee shuffled away, I nodded in the entryway of the minaret rather than ascend its heights. Over the years, I found much succor in that vestibule, in which I took a daily respite for my newly acquired and fulfilling habit.

I never came across any drunkards who used my minaret for their ungodly ministrations. Perhaps the flicker of my lantern was for them a reminder of the fires that awaited in the afterlife!

THE FAMILIALS

Since it cannot be promised that events from our past will be faithfully rendered, I will here note the Three Trials of Ibrahim.

Trial One: Ibrahim and his wife Sarah could not conceive a child, and so his lineage would terminate! For He is the Restricting One.

Trial Two: Ibrahim would be given a son through Sarah's handmaiden Hajar. And then the Lord would ask Ibrahim to behead that very son! For He is the Distressor.

Trial Three: Ibrahim would be asked to deposit Hajar and his firstborn son Ismail in an uncultivated valley outside the Holy Square House with nary a drop of water! For He is the Bestower of Sufficiency.

Ibrahim answered the Lord with a surety that we all must admire but of course, must not idolize. And as a reward, the Lord made Ibrahim and his descendants the establishers of prayer. For He is the Just One.

THE HARVEST GOATS

Through my slow-moving ruse, life at the mosque passed in leisurely toil. As the Lord says: *How sweet the guerdon of the toilers!* I served tea from a pewter tray, stacked rugs, snared vermin, and while the faithful communed with the Lord I arranged the boots and sandals deposited at the mosque's entrances. Perhaps all assumed I was feebleminded and lacked use for pious instruction. Like beasts, the feeble are exempt from His judgment as I understood, so I rarely attended prayer until my aunt's arrival. But, I retained whatever teachings filtered into my tireless mind.

My ministrations aided in harvesting chatter from locals and those coarse men who safeguarded our State through their bloody work. Jay-hawkers were they, Fanatics, dressed in caps and shawls and bandoliers! Inspired by these true hard Kansans, I surveilled the forest, but I did not witness a nest for those Missouri Bushwhackers. When they executed their prosaic terrors on our mosque, I harvested the copper pellets in my pockets. At night, I lit tobacco and devised plots in which I rode a stallion or bull camel and swung a forked sword.

Like the drover, I adapted to the treachery of the Missourians and even the false treachery of the miners. Bombs burst around us but uprooted neither stone nor cedar. Imam Bahira in his Prophet's Day sermons praised the shielding hand of the

Lord, but I suspected that the proximity of a chalk mine and the known ineptitude of the savages could be equally credited.

I remained steadfast in my belief that Bahira, if I may be familiar, could have taken a vigorous roll defending us through judicious interpretation of the Holy Book. Regretfully, the preacher held a suspicion against the sanguinary passages and sermoned instead on covenants, on heifers, on all sorts of natural wonders and how they testified to the Lord's presence. And of course, he spoke on the Lord's ninety-nine names: the Hearer, the Seer, the Everlasting, and on and on as if we had to be convinced. As if the creation of the sun and moon, of our teeming Country, weren't proof enough that we are a blessed people, a blessed land!

And the imam lectured as fakirs do on the coming of a Redeemer who would ride a white horse and slay the menace from the east. A rousing tale that sated the need for scripture to captivate on a wintery afternoon with the mosque bereft of worshippers.

But in truth, who had ever seen a white stallion?

Occasionally, souls tousled my mane as if to say, "there there, my son." I nuzzled against their cracked hands as a feline might. But like many urchins, the faces of my parents eluded me. I saw traces of them in every citizen: those who arrived through the emigrant aid societies and born Kansan alike. For a great while, I scanned the sooty eyes of the mosque's congregants hoping to detect an imperfection that would reveal a man I could call my father. I found none. I liked to believe that if he was, wherever he was, who or whatever he was, he remembered me very much, and my name was always on his lips like a dirge. There were days I would even have settled for a mother.

As I stacked rugs one day, the imam noted that I had the placid demeanor of someone born in an eastern county of our State. I was not certain this was praise—those counties were not far from the imperfect edge of our revered near-rectangle.

In any case, the events surrounding my birth were clouded, insubstantial. Like the individuals I might have called my parents, if ever I had memory of them, I no longer do. This much I knew: I was born in Kansas. It was conceivable that I was made from man. I may have had a mother and a father. Or maybe, as the Lord suggests in the Good Book and I was inclined to believe, I was created from a clot of earth, planted in a glass tube filled with milky minerals, cultivated until limbs sprouted from my torso: Arm, leg, leg, arm. Ha!

But then, and here's where my troubles began, I was harvested too soon by the eager hands that made me. Unfinished. Unripe. My spindly legs wrapped around one another like the roots of a dandelion. And yet, although I was rudely stamped with these deformities, I trusted in the Merciful, the Beneficent. I never hesitated to add my name to the list of Believers, of Partisans, of Whatever It Was We Were Calling Each Other Now Even if They Will No Longer Have Me.

I say all of this to begin correcting a mistake.

The wrong Person has been venerated, and another wrong person, his cousin, has been entombed: forced to spend my remaining days in a crumbling minaret rehashing his and his sanctified mother's stories—even if the veracity of these stories was at best uncertain!

Indeed, mankind is most unjust and ungrateful!

I learned to decipher the hues of the imam's beard. The most important: When pigment leached from the hairs, the color a brittle clay, I slaughtered the harvest goat.

Near dawn, I culled the ripe animal from the pack and enticed it with acorns. After gaining its trust in this devious manner, I slipped a rope around its neck and led it to the shed. Call me a shepherd, if you must.

The next part was the challenge—binding the beast's legs.

Not infrequently, the animal, sensing the blood splatter in the shed, bolted for the mosque, seeking shelter. Because I was not fast, a chase never occurred, and I forfeited that day's allotment if the imam performed the loathsome task. If I was fortunate, which at that early hour was almost never the case, an intrepid worshiper captured the horned escapee so I could finish the process.

With the animal secured, I wrapped its uncooperative legs as it bucked and strained and bleated. I routinely caught a hoof where a bruise would sprout. With the goat's legs bound, I bucked and strained and bleated as I hoisted the beast to the shed's tin ceiling. Then, I turned my palms upward and thanked the Good Lord God the Provider. I placed a pail below the beast's frightened and childlike face, whispered, "there there now," and with a blessed blade drew the line liberating the creature from this world as its succulent flesh fought to remain in it. The red spray that followed soothed my chapped palms. I was fortunate to have bartered my custodial services for a spare tunic, which I employed during the slaughter.

As life drained from the creature into the bucket, I rolled a smoke and intoxicated myself until the beast no longer bucked. Would that we could understand the pleadings of beasts and offer them succor without the use of sharp instruments.

On one occasion, I did attempt to subdue a defiant beast with my meager hands but found the animal adept at occasioning contusions on my person. The Goat of Noble Aspirations, the one who bore me on my arrival to the mosque, caused me no trouble when he visited the shed. I rewarded him with a whetted blade.

With the imam's assistance, I carted the carcasses to the canteen, where we halved and quartered with hacksaw and Wilson blade until the bones were broken down and boiled for stock. We salted and stored what we did not shred in a wheat porridge. In the mornings, the imam fed the birds scraps, and in the evenings, scavengers snatched the festering remnants. Years passed before I saw the hawk that had attacked the imam, but I thought on it often enough as to believe I could summon it.

Each day began for me in my room atop the minaret with its view of stunning Kansas. And each night, I ascended the stone staircase—ninety-nine, one-hundred, one-hundred-one—into my chambers.

THE ASSASSINS

I was given a new name. I did not prefer it. The story was as follows: On land near the Kawsmouth, a horde of Jay-hawker Fanatics concluded a successful, I was certain, raid into Missouri territory. The Kawsmouth was a prime source for fresh water, and its dominion was what much of the ongoing belligerence concerned. It's also the point from which any attempts to rectangularize our State must commence.

As our men returned, they passed through the hilly county north of the mosque, where they were ambushed by Missouri Bushwhackers, perhaps the same ones, we thought, who were tormenting our peoples. Despite having ridden for days, our Fanatics, safeguarded by the Lord, performed the requisite slaughter.

Tragically, one unfortunate caught a blade or a bullet somewhere susceptible. His noble horse found its way to our sanctuary where the rider collapsed in front of my tower and streaked gore across the whitewash. The riderless steed ambled through an archway and into the mosque, where it was confronted by my person.

This was after I sacrificed the Goat of Noble Aspirations, and I was as you may imagine overjoyed to have a new ambling companion—one that was already saddled! I thought about Hajar and Ismail in the uncultivated valley, and how the Lord had provided for them. Was I not as deserving? When Hajar needed water, the Almighty struck a well. When one needed an ambling partner, the Lord provided too!

Also, I was unaware that our Fanatic lay bleeding by the minaret. His lamentations drowned by the droning of evening locusts. Of course, the steed was not willing or able (who can be sure?) to disclose the information.

The imam and devotees were in his office, and I led the snorting creature to the canteen so as not to disturb their reflection. As I have mentioned, I was courteous.

The animal was missing part of an ear, and one of its eyes had clouded over as if it had taken buckshot or birdshot to the face. Herein the cruelty of our rivals was revealed: Who would shoot a horse in the face? A Missourian, that's who.

But the animal was mine, and it stood a full ten if not fifteen hands tall! I stroked its weathered face and fed it grains before I devised a stepstool to mount it. The task was not without complications, but I planted myself on the beast like those famed forefathers of ours. Straddling that creature, I felt purpose bloom in my meager person, and my spine burned with honor and authority. I was certain this was the Prophet's feeling when he rode into B_____ and retook it from the unbelievers.

Although I had seen the trick performed, I miscalculated and faced the ass-end rather than the creature's mane and head and reins. It was a common mistake that bedeviled even the surest of horsemen.

The error, however, put the beast in a fierce mood, and who could have expected that?

Bucking and kicking commenced, and the horse upturned a scalding pot of porridge, which splashed against the animal, narrowly missing me and further enraging it. I clutched its flanks, certain that I would be thrown and would end up wrapped in muslin in the bed of the hearse in which I had arrived!

The animal surged into the prayer hall. You would think
that the Lord would act to preserve His home, but He did
nothing to calm the steed, which toppled prayer rugs, careened
into pillars, crashed water jugs, and urinated wildly!

The commotion roused the imam and his company from
their sequestration. Thankfully, they acted on behalf of or in
lieu of the Lord (who can be certain?), reined the steed and
rescued my flailing person. The imam's beard registered his
displeasure as it did, but I will admit surprise when he yanked
my clammy form from the saddle and clopped me on the ears.
I thought I had been deafened, and my head rang for days.

I was ordered, it should come as no surprise, to undirty the
horse's misdeeds and was disallowed possession of the animal.
And wasn't that punishment enough?

The Fanatic expired at the base of the minaret. You could
not find many who did not blame his passing on my frippery
with the horse. But surely this elevated or denigrated or equated
my status to that of a Missourian terrorist, and that was not a
fair or equitable comparison!

Nevertheless, my new name came about as such: The
body of the man had been cleansed, wrapped, and retrieved by
the squirrel-faced drover, the letters K.U.D. returning to his
overalls, and I restored the canteen and washed the befouled
prayer hall.

Then, I returned to the minaret with lye and bucket and
brush, and I scrubbed and scrubbed at the man's carnage. I
will tell you that my hands still cramp when I recall this Fanatic's viscera and his ability to embed it so thoroughly into the
facade of my dwelling as if his dying request was to ensure that
I enacted a penance for failing to heed his lamentations.

While I cleaned, congregants returned for the evening
prayer. The imam held services in the wrecked field behind the
mosque due to the lingering horse odors inside.

As she passed by me, an elderly covered woman remarked

that I was such a "hard scrubber"—a comment that I did not register as an offense or otherwise, but which provoked giggles from her schoolgirl brood, which I did regard as offensive.

In the ways of these things, the nickname Hard Scrubber took hold. Eventually and because sloth is infectious in our Country, this sobriquet transformed simply into: Scrub. So, when I was addressed at all by the congregants, I was called Scrub as if my given name had no purchase in their imaginations.

Call me Scrub, if you must.

One morning during the Fasting Month that preceded the Festival, a band of our Fanatics rode to the mosque. They were unregenerate and bore a paltry look, even by Bleeding Kansan standards, and you would not be faulted if you mistook them for Bushwhackers! But they wore the sunflower, and it shone on their tunics.

I was scouring the slaughter shed when they arrived, and I tucked my knife into my waistband before trekking to the minaret for a washbasin and water pail.

When I met up with them outside the mosque, I was over-powered by their sour scent, which reminded me of overripe crabapples. Soot encrusted their uniforms, which they beat out. A bandage was wrapped around one's arm, and he seemed to be the superior or at least he conversed with the most grit.

After the men lashed their horses, I scrubbed their feet with a sandalwood soap that we administered on Chieftains from nearby counties. I often employed the soap on myself, but abstained to trail the men, who found audience with the imam. I positioned my duties nearby in hopes of discerning their conversation.

Crickets cried, but I disregarded their nuisance.

From the discord that breached the seclusion, I believe the following was said:

Dignitaries: Your gracious sir, we have returned from a sortie in the land of the pale and peaked!

Imam: Sirs, well done, sirs! May the Lord continue to rain His blessings on our land.

Dignitaries: Thank you, sir. Now that we are here, we do require some assistance.

Imam: May our parish be of assistance to you, as you seek retribution on those who would harm and overrun our peoples?

Dignitaries: We have ascertained that the Accursed have a stronghold northeast of here. We request your people's aid as we root these occupiers from our land!

Imam: Sirs, as the prophet says, *"Whom ye war against, I war against."* We are well positioned, as we are where we are found, well situated to provide your assault with a staging ground. But we are wanting on provisions and the water and milk and the meat and the like.

Dignitaries: Sir, we require more than that: Arms! Men! Horses! Water! Feed! Whatever else you can spare!

Imam: Sirs, while I—while we—are not at the stage to help you and our peoples are not so well-equipped, we will, of course, be certain to assist in your glorious plans.

The imam fled his chambers just as a bomb burst overhead. It rattled the flock of birds that had taken residence inside the mosque. Stone crashed in the prayer hall. But I was unmoved by the commotion, and Bahira barreled into me before he disappeared into the mosque's cellar.

I portioned out tea and with a tray of silver steaming cups entered the imam's chambers where I found the men decamped by the bookshelves—their legs splayed in front of them in a manner unusual to our customs. The Fanatics, who were not abstaining during the Fasting Month due to their travels, seemed unbothered by the unpleasantries that had unfolded. I appraised them of Bahira's whereabouts should they require him. My intention was to manufacture another confrontation in a location better amenable to my reconnaissance.

It took not a moment for me to recognize that these were the types of fellows one would want to assist in the rousting of invaders. Men of character and yes, of industry. I tendered to them my assistance and fealty in their glorious program. I could not promise, I said, that others would join me for there remained an unease regarding my standing amongst our congregation, but my skills would prove useful. Missourians were known cowards. The Lord be praised.

The men thanked me and noted how skilled I was, which was undeniable but seldom appreciated. The bandaged one exclaimed, "If you wield a sword as well as you deliver tea, then Fear Infidels Fear!"

I had not expected the magnitude of their gratitude, and the praise drove me to unsheathe the knife from where it had been pressing into my tenderness. For them, I executed the stabbing and slashing gestures I had practiced in my tower.

The seasoned men howled, and one clapped me across the chest with his pistol! Such respect and honor I can fairly say I have not since reaped.

"Surely," the bandaged one proclaimed, "you will lead our charge!" The others raised their cups in salute. It was a glorious scene.

I will admit surprise at their enthusiasm, but in truth I had earned it, and I had believed I was prepared. I decided to regale them with the story of how I tamed the steed who had wandered into and befouled the mosque, when the imam returned. The brute snatched my scimitar and with my tray, smacked me across the backside and humiliated me in front of my detachment!

Before I could bewail or rouse the others to my defense, the imam ushered me out of his chambers, and my leg braces skittered across the tile. I tried to protest but it was a weak rebellion. I shuffled to the base of my tower where tobacco comforted me. Harsh errands, I thought. Exposed necks supplicating. Head throbbing. The shed would not be washed!

That afternoon, I skulked into the forest behind the minaret where I unleashed a lengthy stream and wandered among the vermin—defenseless I should note.

I heard the bilal call for the midday prayer and made my way back to the mosque where I found the Fanatics' beasts feeding from a trough and citizens congregating for prayer. Despite my reluctance to be in the presence of adherents, I returned to the hall and gleaned a spot near the grizzled men, who had attracted portly admirers. I sat in their remarkable manner with my feet outstretched before me.

The imam recounted a tale of the desert, which, although altered in subsequent years, I have heard many times and will deliver here in its original form:

When assassins crept into his house and marched into his bedchamber, they found him asleep—red or brown hair peeked from beneath ragged covers. They unsheathed their daggers, unhid them from the scarves tied around their waists. Nods passed between them, and each bowed his head in supplicant conspiracy. They agreed: The time was now; it had come to this; it must be done.

The scarves fluttered and snapped as a wind pressed into them. The men feared that he would wake. They held down their garments. For a moment, they did not exhale.

The Prophet remained motionless before them. If he was dreaming, his dream itself was mute, uncolored by thought.

The weapons suddenly large for their hands but not unfamiliar, in unison—as if choreographed in a candlelit, regicidal cave—the four men struck blindly, unleashed strands of words shaped like scythes, and tore up the linens. Feathers and cotton filled the air. The assassins feared that they would strike one another as what felt like blood, a warmth, obscured their eyes. Their weapons guided by impulse alone.

For the moment, in a small room in an indistinct house on the peninsula where language was consecrated and repaired, it snowed on the sand. The room motionless, glacial. Frost heavied the intruder's eyelashes. Their beards icicled and threatened to drop and denude their faces.

The confused men regrouped. Huddled and shuddering, they balanced a new weight fashioned by their flailing and pulled back the torn sheets to find his body gone. There had been no blood shed, no one dismembered or disemboweled, no throat cut, no one silenced.

They searched the remnants of his cot, dug their fingers in, and found that it was warm to the touch. The body that was there lying asleep had left, but its heat remained. At once, the cabal warmed itself on the disembodied heat of the Prophet like a family around a fire, their chapped palms exposed.

The cold flakes and the sheered cotton settled in around them, and they gulped down the air, noticing that they had been unable to breathe. The air in the room bitter—it coated their mouths with a frail salve— before becoming forgiving.

In the congested room, the tired men knelt on the floor, as a man's quiet form appeared. Prone on the bed, not tall, not gaunt, not round, bare-chested but dressed in a white gown that was tucked between his legs. The man collected what he could of the shredded sheets and propped himself up.

Without acknowledging the others that were camped at his feet who massaged their necks and their backs, he returned to sleep as one weary from a long trip, from a taxing excursion to a foreign but hospitable place. If he was dreaming, he continued his dream as though uninterrupted, as though slumber was only dream.

Tomorrow, he will forgive these men, excuse them from his house and *promise that neither they nor their families will be harmed. He will tell them that he understands these are trying times. He will fill their scarves with dates stuffed with almonds and then motion for them to leave. The men will return to their homes, a slight tremor affecting each one's gait, hungry but unable to swallow; their throats dry.*

For the Lord is the Beneficent, the Merciful.

"Learn a lesson, O ye who have eyes!" I wanted to howl after the imam had finished his tale about the assassins. As if we needed further sermonizing to discern the particular failings of this so-called priest and his chicken-hearted ways.

The blaze in me ceased to untemper.

The grizzled Fanatics filed out after prayers, and again I trailed them. Perhaps there was a kinship between those who have been and are currently bandaged: The wrapped Fanatic heeded my malingering and motioned for me to assist with his horse.

"You'll shepherd this mosque one day," he growled. "And when you do, be sure to send word. We'll need you then."

I offered him my hand.

The men saddled and rode and engulfed me in a cloud of dust and expectations. I thought of the blimp, that fat gorgeous creature. The blimp swirled in my head.

Goats licked the salt from my face, my hands. I would eat them, I thought, were I not abstaining.

THE MINERS

The bandaged Fanatic stoked in me a base appetite that would not be satiated without the departure of a certain father.

And along with that appetite came many questions: What was, in fact, our purpose if not to safeguard our peoples? To protect a lineage that had survived torments both manmade and those forged by the Lord Himself! For is the Lord not also the Retaliator? Should we not, at the very least, aspire to inhabit His many names? To honor the Lord by enacting His presence here in our Country?

Was I not ordained for a greater purpose than mosque custodian and goat slaughterer? If I inherited the mosque, I could retell our stories! Fashion them to best aid our glory, our conquest over those who sought our State for their infidel extravagances.

But how did one execute such a conspiracy? Would I, like those Assassins of Yore, find my eyes covered in blood and my nascent beard frosted over like a pasture at dawn? Did blood shed in the name of liberty stain its practice? Surely it did not! The Lord be praised.

And how did one cultivate the mettle to dispatch an unwanted clergyman? I was certain that such fortitude, like those hardy herds that sustained us, required careful and proper husbandry.

I did what any devotee would do to seek guidance or develop a stratagem: I scoured the Holy Book, stacks of which I had ferreted in my cloister. And I encountered the Wise and All-Knowing Verses: *For does not the Lord say there are those who put up a mosque by way of mischief and infidelity to disunite the Believers. The Lord declares that they are certainly liars.*

"*Liar*" was what the Book called him! Deserving then of the ultimate retribution, which would be discharged by my calloused hands!

I resolved that I would undertake this labor in a manner befitting a stalwart Fanatic—a hard veteran of Kansas! I was all on fire for it. No deployment of the word "son" would sway me from my chosen task! Unlike my commonplace duties at the mosque, I would hold steadfast. I would develop and deploy the grotesque plot to annex the mosque and spearhead our long-awaited crusade against the Missourians—for the glory of our people and our Lord! *For verily the Almighty is with the steadfast!*

If God was for us, then who could be against? The Lord be praised!

And yet, I regret to tell you that a season passed in its milky manner, the Festival to the harvest, before I formulated a plan. Always distracted by something on the periphery. For is He not also the Delayer?

Despite my initial fervor, I found a fulfilling diversion by tormenting our congregants, many of whom feared that savage Missourians or the spirits of those who had perished at their hands haunted our forest! You could not say that we lived among the uninspired.

It was rather effortless for me to profit on their distress even with the primitive trickery afforded me. I harvested stones and by lamplight hurled them from the portal in my tower, which startled nesting vermin who then scampered into the prayer hall as worshippers communed with the Lord. The shrieks I elicited! *But it was the Lord that threw*, I thought....

My grandest scheme, unexecuted but not unimagined, was as follows: As winter advanced and the oak shed their verdure, I accompanied that base man, the squirrel-faced drover—not the imam—on a water pilgrimage. Into quilts, I wrapped hardtack, salt goat, and chicory. I then loaded our provisions, as well as the spent water barrels, into the bed of the cart. The five-legged steer drove our precarious forms as we clattered north into rolling country that, like much of our State, was to me unexplored.

As if we had reached an agreement to remain silent, though we had not, the drover and I exchanged little. When we stopped for prayers, I made certain to rinse upstream of him. I refrained from tobacco in his presence, for fear that he might uncover my earlier treachery, and that was a task as challenging as others I have faced, so used to the custom had I grown.

The day drained as I lolled in the bed of the familiar cart and attempted to devise a method to dispatch the imam. Plots such as these, I was certain, came to no one easily or there would have been insurrections, rebellions, and uprisings fortnightly. Nothing very uncommon, I suppose.

A pair of blasts, which startled only the five-legged beast, portended our arrival at a limestone quarry. The drover halted the cart on a bluff that overlooked the drudgery of our prospectors, who thundered away, blasting and retrieving. They scurried with handcarts, hauling stone, powdered in an alabaster dust as if aping Massachusetts men. The sun bleached them in a brilliance that would, in time, render the miners sightless.

My own industry was—and I suspected would always be—tinged with a cripple's inertia. Not theirs.

While we gnawed on jerky, the drover and I watched a pair of miners haul a powder cask into a cave. They ran a long fuse, lit it, and then fled. A salvo followed that rattled the bluff and scattered chirrs.

These casks, I surmised, could execute the grim task I

needed done if I was to wrest control of the mosque. But how to acquire the munitions, I wondered? The question bedeviled me. *Wait patiently for the fulfillment of thy Lord's decree*, I thought. Then, the heavy rain came and scared us beneath a tarp. But soon enough it quit, and it was again scorching. If there was one constant in my life, it was the indecipherability of our weather!

I slumbered that night in the cart bed while the drover dozed on his bench. The next day found us fields where feral camels broke, past the hogback ridge, which the Bush-whacking terrorists had once used as a staging ground—their sulfur lingered still!—and finally we met the remnants of our once-bursting metropolis.

I spied the river market, and it was deserted save for those brave cattlemen. Where were the clanging hammers? The choking smoke?

The factories that had crowded the riverbanks had been emasculated—their smokestacks removed and repurposed. At least one had been transformed into a minaret.

Then, we were into disputed lands—the northeast corner of our State, the very direction we prayed, where the sinewy Missouri River crooked and waggled and complicated our earnest perimeter.

Of the many advantages of our land—a central location, unsullied rivers, proximity to glorious Colorado and that State's ceaseless springs—its shape was not one of them. You would remember that the Creator abhors disharmony, and that seeking His favor Mahometans erected their dwellings and houses of worship in exacting symmetry. It was why, no doubt, our Kansas took the form of a near rectangle, a shape second only to the steadfast square in its glorious design. The Missouri River's bend made a mockery of our sincerity. And it would not surprise you to learn that this disfigurement served as a border with those Missourian Pukes. (A scar that will be rectified by my cousin's minions in the blood and treasure of so many of their wretched—the Lord be praised!)

When finally the drover and I found the riverbank, it was fortified: Cannons thundered from the Kawsmouth. Rain came by way of dirt, showering us in country and scattering other water pilgrims who, in their threadbare denim and tattered tunics, clutched their grim children and clambered for a drink.

Thanks to the Lord for sheltering me from them. For a time, at least.

The drover guided us downstream of the warring to the inviolable, although languid, Kansas River. We had already wrangled our barrels, filled and sealed them and then prepped for our return, when we saw Bushwhackers parading a half-dozen of our Jay-hawker Fanatics, the sunflowers wilted on their lapels, across the river from Kaw Point.

All stopped their harvesting to gawk at the spectacle: Our men had been blindfolded, and their hands bound behind them.

The Bushwhackers led them into a defile and out of sight, but in view of the river market. Though we could not see them, we heard the Bushwhackers sermon: "We shall slay you even as Ad and Iram were slain." The words broke across the river and died on our shore. The next thing we heard was the report of pistols, the wailing of our men, the wailing of the river market denizens and then silence. Gunsmoke lifted into the vault. It was a slaughter, and if we needed further proof of the depredations of our foes—which we did not—we had it.

If the execution was meant to cause restraining fear, it did just that. There was no insurrection of our people, instead they fled, and again cannons thundered.

The slaughter of our men sombered me. Had I lost the very Fanatics to whom I had sworn my allegiance? Could this loss have been averted had we simply assisted the men who had come to ask for our assistance? And where was our cavalry?

Lo, I was certain these were not times for chicken-hearted leaders! If there was one thing I knew, it was how to truss and slay beasts! And if there was more of a beast than a Bush-whacker, I would not have wanted to meet it!

I dug my feet into the muck, which seemed to suck the warmth right out of me. Our people required a sure hand if we were to persist. Not the leader we had, but the leader *I* would become. The bloodwite would be repaid by the shedding of Infidel blood! We would pave our trails with their crushed skulls! For the Lord is the Avenger!

I sidled next to the drover, who removed his cap. We both mumbled a prayer: *To Him we shall return….* And then, as he sucked his teeth, he again rasped out: "*To Him we shall return….*" We quit for the cart and rode back to the mosque to inform, educate, and execute.

To the joy of the worshippers, our return swelled the cistern. But the revelry was momentary, then muted. The drover revealed the slaughter we had witnessed to the imam. And to his credit, at the next Prophet's Day sermon Bahira recalled the savagery, versions of which had already spread through the congregation. As I have said, our citizens were far from unimaginative. The Lord be praised!

But having witnessed the massacre, I grew uninterested in the gossip—of how the savagery's particulars transformed from teller to told. Instead, I fixated on the miners' blasting kegs, which occupied my cagey and unkempt mind. I was desirous of them with an appetite that surpassed even my cravings for smoke and meat porridge.

And the Almighty was with the steadfast! I waited some might say patiently until one day a band of miners arrived in a laden bullock cart. Why they delayed the delivery of their cargo to congress with the worshipful, I was not certain. Was not demolition a form of prayer? For is He not also the Destroyer?

A tarp obscured the contents of their cart, but when the

prospectors ambled into the prayer hall, I set down my broom and explored the treasures I was meant to not see. The cover had been lashed to the cart bed with such craft that when I released the knots with only a few quick-fingered motions, I nearly scraped into the mosque and sought accolades. But I staunched that appetite.

The kegs unveiled, each bantam, black-powdered barrel testified to my conspiracy. A locust landed on a keg as I inhaled the beguiling aroma of decayed fowl eggs, rich poison, and promise!

But the kegs hid their heft. I eased a barrel off the cart, and it bashed me into the gravel. After righting myself, I rolled the keg to the base of my tower, before I re-lashed the tarp to conceal my machinations.

I joined the worshippers at the rear of the prayer hall and placed myself within sight of the imam—for I knew the meaning of the word deception and it was conformity. If the miners noticed my pilfery, it was never brought to my attention. I suspected that in their earnest industry, they must have consumed black powder by the bale-full and that kegs vanished like untended tobacco.

That evening, when the worshippers all had departed and my false father had retired, I lugged the keg into my chambers one protesting step at a time. Remarkably, when sweat-drenched I arrived into my room, only a slight trail of powder followed. I found a lucifer and with a flash, with a flash the grains were gone.

The miner's keg remained swaddled in a quilt in my chambers—undeployed but not forgotten. The twin difficulties of manufacturing a ruse and executing said ruse without damaging the mosque beset my ambitions. *I must only burn the town and have the blood*, I thought.

But no, my failure to liberate the mosque from that Bahira was not from a lack of ambition or even of appetite for certain ill deeds. Just as I had acquired the mechanism for my ascendancy, immigrants—let us not forget that despite the reverence afforded them in our State, that my cousin and his mother were unnative to our land—immigrants from somewhere far and inhospitable arrived into our congregation. Invited as they were by the imam himself. And perhaps the Lord.

And is this not what you've been waiting to hear? The tales of Faisal, not of F_____? The stories of my cousin and his mother? The monstrous and phenomenal situation of his birth? And of the circumstances that delivered him and my aunt to our Country?

Secretly, you curse me for having made you wait so long to hear them—the volumes on your shelves incomplete without an account of their fables!

And so, you will have it.

I have pieced together many of the stories that follow from gossip and careless chatter I overheard between prayers. Others were told to me by my aunt, as on occasion I did swath her feet in warm towels. And yes, still others were sung to me by Ms. A_____, when she took up the lyrical arts and sere-naded us at the coffeehouse. I have heard these tales so often, they have kept me so much company these past years, that I have come to inhabit them as if the characters were bound to me by more than just blood. I have come to think of these stories as my own. Would that they were.

THE LIGHT

A cannon, she thought, a cannon.

As she awaited her attendant, my Aunt Maryam rested on a canvas cot, her head and knees high and her belly protruding. She was draped in sheets cleansed with lavender oil, and the scent cocooned and comforted her.

Although she had been stitched, a crimson glow emanated from between her legs. Steam lifted from a washbasin, and a pile of rent cloth lay beside her on the silt floor.

Unease took hold of my aunt. Her husband was absent, his bedroll was missing from the hard cot beside hers. Would he return to see the birth of his second child? She hoped. Years since, she had born him a daughter, Alfiya, named for the first letter of an alphabet she'd been taught as a child. My aunt had been young, and the pregnancy left her with no milk for the infant. My uncle, a diviner by trade who instead peddled religious wares in Y_____'s central bazaar when the wells dried up, could not afford a nursemaid.

Alfiya: whose dark locks grayed in advance of her first birthday; whose mewling ceased from resignation rather than weakness; who was buried in a plot that my uncle dug; whose hillside grave was marked by a slab of unetched black stone that was indistinguishable from those around it save for its diminutive size.

My uncle's clan, ascetics who lived on the outskirts of Y_____, shunned my aunt after Alfiya's passing. When she shuffled by them on her way to the bazaar, they called her "Maryam the Milkless," unconcerned that she might have overheard their abuse.

When thoughts of her first child haunted her, Maryam consoled herself that at least it had not been the infection that had taken her daughter. The town of Y_____ had been decimated by a plague that blistered folks with boils shaped like wildflowers. The town's healers, who counted no fewer than one, one-armed doctor among their numbers, bound oil-soaked cloth to their faces to blunt the smell as they consigned their patients' contagious bodies to a fiery pit.

My uncle feared the pregnancy would once again deplete his wife and that she would need a nursemaid's services. He left to sell his curios in the trading town of B_____. He swore to return only when he had "recovered such sums as would cover any unforeseen eventualities with which the Lord, in his infinite wisdom, may see fit to bless us. We are all Ayyub's children after all." After leaving Y_____ in his mule cart, he and his slave girl were not seen again.

My aunt's second child—who would be known as our Savior—began pushing sooner than expected, and a light beamed from beneath the folds of her dressing gown. It was at first no larger than the timid glow of a firebug lost in the dense cluster of bees between her legs. But as days passed, it grew to the brightness of a candle's flame and flickered with the beat of the child's limbs against her belly. Its brilliance forced my aunt to layer in robes and sleep with winter shawls tucked between her thighs, to obscure the flame from seduced insects.

One stifling night, Maryam awoke to an uncertain sound, like rustling leaves or whispering. Perhaps her husband had returned, and as she lifted from the cot, the shawls fell away. Her aura lighted the tent and scared off shadows. Drawn to her flame, moths circled and formed above Maryam a haphazard halo.

On the floor before her, a clot of ink-black scorpions snapped and hissed. They blocked her path to the cowhide flap of the doorway. My aunt choked with fear. Her breath—she was certain it was her last—caught in her throat as if she had swallowed a stone.

But the creatures recoiled from my aunt's brilliance, and Maryam advanced, dreading their strikes at every moment. The mercenaries encircled her but came no closer than the rose-hued border.

Maryam took a reassured breath and spun slowly around. She surveyed the beasts and thought of Habakkuk, of his many questions to the Lord. As she spun, the scorpions skittered, maintaining their distance at the edge of her light. She took small but more confident steps and twirled to the mottled cowhide, escorted by her hissing companions. They danced around her as if making reverent tawafs. The scorpions struck at my aunt's glow, and venom trailed to the floor in salvos of sparkling droplets.

(Such was said to be the origin of the dervish. When the devout reached their blissful state, and The Beloved grasped them, they were said to gasp "Oh Maryam" in tribute.)

When my aunt arrived outside, the invaders scattered. She swatted away the halo of moths, spat, and tied tight the tails of her black headscarf under her chin like a tourniquet.

My aunt and her husband's clan endured the wildflower plague in shanties that formed a crescent on the eastern slope of town. Her scornful neighbors had gathered before their tents and sod-framed houses to gawk into the distance where a tornado or a sandstorm, lighted by the dual exclamations of lightning and the sliver moon, lurked at the edge of Y_____. A braid of smoke from the pyre spiraled up into the storm. They could see that the men had broken in all directions to drive tent-spokes into uneven soil, dump out grain-filled gunnysacks and bind the fabric between the curtains of grass that passed for walls.

Maryam's neighbors, preoccupied with preparations for the onslaught, failed to notice the light that seeped from her. Though my aunt, for her part, crossed her legs.

In the morning, when they discovered that no gypsum covered the water pails, no hill of silt where the wells stood, their piles of wheat and corn unperturbed, the residents of Y_____ felt that the Good Lord had blessed them by turning the storm. And they flooded Him in prayer. For is He not the Beneficent, the Merciful?

My aunt did not fall back into sleep that night. She had no gunnysacks to empty, no one to help her batten down. The hide that sealed her tent had flapped in staccato gusts, and the tent had lurched and strained on its iron pegs. As she laid on her cot, shawls once again tucked between her legs, she came to a single conclusion: that she must be stitched.

Although she attributed the whisper that woke her and even the swarm of scorpions to the storm, she was certain that the glow from this child was doing more harm than good and attracted creatures of the night. Even if it had been the light that had held the creatures at bay, it would have to be extinguished. She called upon the only doctor who would see a woman who had no husband, a man known as Abedin, who was no more a doctor than a man who saved his physician brother from a wildcat by hacking off that brother's entrapped arm.

At the appointed time, he arrived at Maryam's tent and asked to enter. The balding Abedin unwrapped the soot-streaked cloth that shielded his face. He was the first man to see my aunt without the company of her husband. Inside the tent, the doctor told her to lie down, then lifted the coarse fabric of her dressing gown.

My aunt's glow reflected from Abedin's waxen pate. In an

effort not to appear unschooled, the doctor forced any expression of surprise from his face as he patted down my aunt's dress. Then he stood and picked at a raw spot on his lower back, distracted by his conviction that the more hair he lost above, the more his body compensated by seeding it in less obvious places.

Abedin stared into my aunt's eyes and declared that the child must be sealed in, "held until ready to see the light of the days." It was in ways the reverse of the procedure he had so desperately performed on his brother with a ready hatchet. Nevertheless, Abedin was certain he could perform the task with steady hand, thick needle, and coarse thread.

Prudently placed stitches sealed in my fledgling cousin, and he revolted at the incarceration. He pounded out a furious rhythm on his mother and forced her into a wicker rocking chair for the Festival.

While her neighbors floated past in their thin raiment, my gravid aunt sat as still as a corpse in a garlanded bier and hoped the little bull would take her cue and settle himself. Her position fixed in the chair outside her tent, she watched the days grow shorter as she read from an illustrated Holy Book, which her husband had left. It was unlike any other scripture she had seen: Images of the revered Prophet, scenes of treaties and of battles, of prayer and sermon, painted in fine detail with a camel-hair brush, accompanied the calligraphed text, which peaked and troughed like waves across the pages. The book's edges lacquered in gold, it was a Good Book fit for a grand religion, Maryam thought.

She recited the prayers, propelled the words into her growing flesh and hoped they would reach her little bull. She issued sentence after sacrosanct sentence as though to pierce herself with the words, drive them into her captive son and fill the nascent wells of his ears.

The itchy spots on Abedin's lower back soon bloomed into

wildflowers, and weeks after visiting my aunt, his body was consigned to the flames. A man with only one arm threw his weeping self onto the pyre, and so in one mournful evening, the shantytown of Y_____ lost two of the men who dared to call themselves doctors.

A young midwife named Talib became my aunt's caretaker thereafter. Maryam had called upon the suddenly busy midwife and explained her delicate situation. She promised Talib that upon her husband's imminent return she would "receive such great sums that you will thank the Almighty that you have delivered this child."

If Talib was aware that Maryam's husband had been missing for the better part of a year, she did not reveal it. Instead, she insisted on performing the delivery, "out of a keen curiosity for what it is that you have within, be it god or monster."

When my aunt's travails began, she called out to her neighbors. In an act of charity wholly out of keeping with their natures, they retrieved the inquisitive midwife. The death of this child, they thought, would not fall on them.

Midwife Talib clutched her satchel and on the way to my aunt's tent passed a plump man who cried and took on, as if he encouraged onlookers to join him. His carriage lurched long after the salt from his eyes had ceased to flow, and veins protruded from the man's skin, visible beneath his tattered shirt. Midwife Talib recognized him. She had delivered him a daughter, though the girl and her mother were unseen.

Inside Maryam's tent, Talib set her satchel on the floor next to the strips of rent cloth. Maryam's light streamed forth like a miner's headlamp. While the glow had been diminished by Abedin's handiwork, it had not been extinguished. That it had returned with a still greater brilliance as she neared labor was, my aunt thought, an omen of the child's good health, if nothing else.

The midwife uncovered the breechcloth, shielded her eyes

and searched for the coarse knots that caged my cousin. She found them intact, smiled at her ward, and then rinsed her hands in the steaming bowl.

Propped on the cot, Maryam felt no discomfort, but this worried her. Caused by or an answer to this disquiet, her legs cramped. Though she was relieved to feel pain of a sort, she feared her son would sour—a "little lemon-faced boy" they'd call him. She fretted away her fruitless thoughts as best she could.

She sweated, and her damp face strained as her bull bucked. Relief flooded Maryam's face. The midwife blotted her brow with a pilling rag and tossed it to the floor. She secreted the long black braid of her hair under her headscarf. With another rag, the midwife mopped the sweat from her own face. She fetched scissors from her satchel and again lifted the cloth and felt the thread in the woman before her. Maryam's face contorted in the long blades.

In the days before his mother assumed her role, she was simply Maryam, Auntie Maryam. His mother. My purported aunt.

The midwife braced herself against the cot. She crouched and dropped her shoulder to await the little bull. The heat of Maryam's light blazoned her face but brought with it a surprising comfort like a breeze atop a hillock. With a sharp inhale, Talib snipped my aunt's threads.

A wriggling little boy burst forth and slid across the cot. Cord and knot in hand, he wielded them like a lasso to rope the calf of his mother's placenta as he skittered off the cot, through the midwife's arms, the little greasy bull fell into the pile of cloth, landing with a thud like a spinning coin into a furrowed palm. Tails.

Not a sound escaped from my infant cousin—a rag having found its way into the recesses of his mouth. The midwife snatched him by the skin of his back, her arm braceleted in plum-colored cord. She freed him with another snip and then slapped him—an action that expelled the offending cloth and incited a shriek from the offended boy.

The midwife, disappointed that it was just another human child and not a monstrous winged creature, presented the little bull to his mother. Maryam stroked his back between the shoulder blades where the midwife's fingers left welts, the only blemishes on his golden skin.

This was the resolute child, the strong child, she thought, and named him after a king she once heard of—Faisal. Into his ears, she whispered, "There is no God but the Lord above, and the Prophet is His messenger."

My aunt heard galloping horses, though it was only the clatter of her happy heart. Between her legs, blood bruised the lavender-scented sheets.

This story was sung to me by Ms. A_____ from Y_____.

SHE OF THE INVIOLABLE MILK

With child and with no trade to ply, Maryam was a burden on the reeling community of Y_____, already taxed by the ravages of disease that swept unchecked through its rings.

My aunt's pregnancy had given her a son but had seemingly deprived her of a husband, a grim equation that did nothing to raise her status in the eyes of my uncle's clan. As the infection had made many widowers, she thought she might remarry. But without a way to confirm her husband's death, no man would wed her for fear of his imminent return.

Although Midwife Talib had not divulged the peculiar condition of her charge's pregnancy and birth, the townsfolk grew suspicious of the infant Faisal, who cried so infrequently that they would drop into Maryam's tent unannounced in hopes of interrupting the lonely woman as she did away with the child, drowned him in a deep amphora or beat him tied up alive in a gunnysack. But each time, they found the radiant boy unblemished save for the ink spots between his shoulders.

Maryam believed that upon his birth the light that had streamed from her now coursed through him. It filled the child's heart and imparted a bronze-colored tinge. The midwife assured her that this discoloration would fade as the child flourished.

And he would flourish, for this time Maryam's pregnancy brought her milk.

But it was by no means certain or assured. In the days following my cousin's birth, Maryam's breasts were again dry. The hungry infant would suckle and struggle, and then finally quit as if deceived, having been tricked into the act of feeding. My aunt feared that soon she would have to dig a new grave alongside the one her husband had made for their daughter. She knotted her hands together, ashamed that her body had brought her a son only to abandon him.

As the weeks progressed, the child weakened. His eyes clouded, and the knots of his knees grew wider than his spindly legs. Each night, my aunt dabbed a poppy seed salve on Faisal's gums to ease his thirst and soothe him to sleep. He suckled at the empty air as though he could draw sustenance from it.

To nourish him, Maryam traded away for goat's milk what was left of her husband's belongings: prayer mats, beads, splintered crosses, rosaries, shrouds, and palmwood chewing sticks. Their tent became more and more barren. My aunt bartered my uncle's threadbare cot, his leathers, his acacia pipe, even the scissors he'd used to trim his beard.

At last, she was left with his most prized possession—the illustrated Holy Book, given to him by a maternal granduncle, who had painted the pages. My aunt fingered the sash of satin that bisected the jaundiced paper and pulled open the book. The verses read: *"But they did hamstring her. So, he said: 'Enjoy yourselves in your homes for three days. Then will be your ruin. Behold, there a promise not to be belied!'"*

Illustrated below was a picture of rotund chieftains dismembering a camel. To Maryam, the verses were not comforting, but the story did reward Saleh and the believers.

She bore the last of her husband in her hands as if it were a hefty child, not the ones she had carried. Beside her, Faisal whimpered in the nest of straw that served as his crib. Maryam bound the infant to her back with a twist of his swaddling blanket and delivered the Holy Book to the shepherd's stall at the bazaar. The shepherd's son, a lanky boy whose bare, pigeon-chest was mercifully unblemished by the telltale welts, fingered its pages. Manure from his fingernails streaked the maroon leather binding.

My aunt set Faisal nearby, on a bale of hay. His tiny fingers curled around hers with a strength that belied his deprivation. Maryam searched her son's eyes for a reason why the child had suddenly become so demanding. "Little bull," she asked, "what troubles you?"

In the caverns of his eyes, Maryam thought she could see the branches of a lone acacia tree twisting on the wind. It was well known to everyone and stood outside the gates of the city. Maryam, in her marriage caravan, had passed it on the way to meet her betrothed.

Faisal's long lashes entranced my aunt. She spent hours staring into his eyes, darker than her own, an almond color inherited from his absent father. Sometimes she saw in them fields of mustard flowers. Other times, rolling pastures, and less frequently a sprawling tenement on the outskirts of Y_____.

My aunt peered again into her son's eyes. The clouds had returned, but she could still make out within them the thorny tree. She pressed her child to her chest and snatched the book from the shepherd's son. A page tore away. Fluttering in the attendant's soiled hand was Ibrahim, dutifully pressing his scythe into Ismail's neck.

Child and book in hand, Maryam stumbled through the bazaar. The town had begun to stir amid the tumult of roosters. Sunlight broke between the buildings to parse the path that led to the town center—the council's residence, the lender's office, the shuttered bath, the coffeehouse, a temple, the mosque. She passed fowls hanging from hooks, an ice seller chiseling blocks, a perfumery that reeked of spilled jasmine. Maryam spotted the empty plot where her husband had sold his curios between the furrows of a farmer's stand. She pictured him there, folding a prayer rug. Teeth stained vermillion.

A call rang out from the minaret as the bells clanged from a steeple. Each competed for an audience amid the morning's clatter.

Orienting herself by the smoke, Maryam headed to the funeral pyre. The tracks of bullock carts fleeing the tainted town gouged the trail. She followed the path out through the town's gate and balanced the squirming boy and the illustrated Book.

Hajar, she thought, at least had Gibreel to guide her.

The hike to the acacia led her beyond the pyre. Maryam did not know when the last immolation had taken place, but the ground stank of burning hair. She mistook a charred tree branch for a child's scorched leg, and she hurried her steps, whispering, *"To Him we belong, and to Him we shall return."*

My aunt labored up the slight knoll where the tree grew, tall and austere against the dun-colored hills. Like the esteemed Lote Tree, the acacia was for the people of Y_____ the ultimate demarcation, the last vestige of civilization before the expanse of wilderness and desert, stone and sediment that isolated the town. She fanned herself with her headscarf and laid her son and the Holy Book on a jute mat at the base of the tree. She wondered who had left the mat there, and whether the visit had brought them solace. My aunt scanned Faisal's eyes for a clue as to what to do next. But he'd grown tired and lolled around on his back, trying to capture his elusive feet.

Maryam rooted in the dry silt looking for she did not know what. She rolled up an edge of the mat. Then grabbed the shortest branch and shook it, half-expecting milk to trickle like sap from the hollow thorns and drip into her son's mouth. She succeeded only in startling a pair of roosting doves. Rain came by way of the tree's threadlike flowers, which caught in her hair.

Maryam cursed her foolishness. In her despair, she had dragged her two most precious possessions far afield from the safety of the town. One feeble with hunger, the other despoiled by filth. Here she was, their protector, teetering. What belief had led her here?

She sat at the base of the tree and took the child in her lap. The Book, latticed in white flowers, rested beside her. She brushed petals from Faisal's curls and leaned against the tree, where a single thorn, where no others could be seen, stuck her. When she plucked it aside, red ants bit her.

In the distance, the walls of the town were a ridge indistinguishable from the furthest hills. She palpated the sites of her insults. Then, in what she thought would be a last, futile attempt to feed the boy, Maryam brought Faisal to her chest. The child nursed with the expected lack of success, but as she drew him away, Maryam's nipple shed a pearl tear. The infant continued to feed, revived by the sudden appearance of a new, salty sap. Maryam lay beneath the acacia with the boy at her breast until she ached.

Sated, the little bull fell into an uncolored sleep. Maryam sat with Faisal in her lap under the acacia, elated at her fortune. She was loath to leave until he had fed once more, lest the milk dry up as suddenly as it had appeared.

From her vantage on the knoll, Maryam spied a caravan leaving through the town's gate, which had fallen from its hinges as though the residents now welcomed its enemies—the town was its own pestilent weapon.

A covered wagon was piled with the belongings of several families: chairs, rolls of carpets, bedding, and rusted tent pegs poked from within. Flanked by their wretched parents, sleepy, sandy-haired children dangled their arms from inside of the cart. Oxen trundled forward. All proceeded in silence but for the beasts' grunts and the scraping of boots across the dry land.

Maryam counted fifteen men, most in coarse black suits despite the heat. Others wore long white gowns like her husband had. The women in bonnets or draped headscarves. As they herded past the pyre, the travelers crossed their chests.

Others exhaled prayers for the dead. At least one broke into sobs that echoed off the hills.

My aunt covered herself and adjusted Faisal's blanket to shade him from the sunlight. Blood from a chafed nipple bloomed on her pale gown. As the group passed, they tipped the wide brims of their hats or touched fingers to foreheads in greeting.

One beardless, heavyset man broke from the pack and scampered up the knoll. As he approached, Maryam pulled her headscarf forward and tucked the sides behind her ears.

"Are you all right, ma'am?" he asked and proffered his water-skin. With a shirtsleeve, he dabbed at his sunken eyes. She thanked him, declined his offer and stroked Faisal's sleeping face.

"Forgive me for asking, but is your child still unweaned?" he pried. She nodded in assent. "I have a baby, a daughter," he said. "She is sick. All of Y_____ is sick. And now my wife is gone." He gestured toward the pyre and snaked a meaty finger up to the sky.

"I am sorry for you, for your child," replied my aunt, who scanned the caravan for the desperate man's daughter. "They leave you," she added.

"They move slowly," he countered, and they watched the sorry group crawl forward. "We are many families. Or parts of families. Perhaps families of parts." He paused for a moment to watch the migrants.

"If you are OK, then I can go," he said and tucked his shirt into his trousers where it strained against his girth.

As he left, he asked, "Might you nurse my daughter? I could pay you."

Maryam flushed at the man's question and readjusted her scarf. Faisal slumbered, and she recalled a passage from the Good Book, *"Beware of the day when no soul will help another soul."*

Thus compelled, she replied, "please bring me your child."

The stout man threaded through the dispirited procession

to retrieve his daughter. Maryam lay the sleeping Faisal on the jute mat and took the girl in her embrace.

This was the infant Ms. A_____!

She was larger than Maryam's son, older by weeks, and her listless eyes had clouded like his had. Maryam quickly inspected the child, searching for boils, welts, or other sores, but finding none she asked the man to, "Please, please turn away." He descended to the base of the knoll, watching the caravan as it rounded a hillock, out of sight.

My aunt pressed herself to the girl's shriveled mouth. Maryam thought of her first born, Alfiya, as she snuck a kiss onto the girl's hirsute forehead. Wind rustled the acacia, and flowers spiraled on her and the child, who fed until she, like the infant boy beside her, grew sleepy.

Maryam composed herself. Upon seeing his child satiated in my aunt's arms, the man fell prostrate and wept. He shook and lurched with each cry as if he were a fat cow undone by slaughter. His wail caromed off the surrounding hills and flooded Y_____ with the lamentations of joy. My aunt thought that she had heard this peal once before, perhaps in a slightly different key, though she could not place it.

(What overcame this man, the imam has said, was the pure truth of divinity: When confronted with the divine, even mundane acts such as wet-nursing transform the mere believer into a zealot.)

After he had recovered from his paroxysm of joy, the man raced to the caravan and with his stoutness blocked the oxen, forcing the group to a halt. The beasts swatted flies with their tails. A crow called.

"I—I have met her!" he stammered. "She of the inviolable milk." He recounted his story and urged those with children to stay and build a camp in the shade of the acacia, outside the infected town.

Most berated him and shouted "Fool, do you think the

defilement will not find you there?" and "Leave us to our journey! Your sorrow has disabled your sense!"

But the parts of families, the men without wives or children, the women without husbands or sons, the urchins without parents, heeded the plump man's call. His wail had pierced their bony chests, made them wonder what unfettered joy could come in this time of calamity.

"We will build our own well," the man promised, "we will speak the pure language of the hills. We will be untainted!" He preached those folks right into my aunt's arms.

The Family of Parts, as the earliest adherents were called, reclaimed their belongings along with their children. They said farewell to the others, eliciting more rebukes, "May the infection burst your children and their children!" and the man returned to my aunt with the former townsfolk.

The women of the Family were first to reach Maryam. They bore their children in their arms and across their backs, and my aunt took the infants to her breast as the women surrounded her and formed a living wall of privacy. Seen from the gates of Y_____, a battalion of sturdy women protected the acacia, whose branches burst from inside their tight circle.

The men of the Family set up camp at the foot of the knoll. Led by the plump man, they fetched Maryam's belongings and handed her tent to the women, who sliced into the canvas so that when it was finally pitched, the acacia sprung from the center of the tent. All the while, my aunt sat on the jute mat exchanging one sickly infant for the next, her breasts sore but not dry.

Maryam's former neighbors had now a barren space between their homes, thankful that their burden had relocated, as indifferent to the location as they were to her husbandless presence.

The early weeks of the Family passed for my aunt in this manner: Unless she slept or tended her own boy, she fed another's child. The infants, often unsightly, increasingly older, clamped onto her breasts and scraped their teeth over her flesh. In the morning, Maryam applied a buttermilk and poppyseed salve to soothe her breasts as she once had to Faisal's gums.

Word of my aunt's fortitude spread through the beleaguered town. Soon, even those who had called her Maryam the Milkless would call her by the name with which the plump Family man had blessed her: Maryam of the Milk. My aunt's wards would include a patriarch afflicted with the doldrums, a grandmother hobbled by gout. Her women acted as both her keeper and her servants. They insisted she heal as many as she could and chased away only those who sprouted wildflower blisters.

The grateful left tributes of hard honey candy, lavender oil, and barley bread, or they fetched her water and hoisted the earthenware pots atop their heads to amuse my aunt. They sewed her garments or patched her dressing gowns and scrubbed stains with a cornstarch paste.

Maryam and Faisal thrived beneath the acacia in this manner, attended to by the Family of Parts. Faisal's first steps found him stumbling from his mother's arms to the tree's trunk. After his circumcision, performed by Midwife Talib, the women of the Family garlanded him with the tree's flowers.

Clouds hovered over the knoll so that the Family of Parts was doubly covered in shade from the creeping branches of the acacia and by the fog. They tilled the adjacent hillock and ventured into the sick town of Y_____ only for trade. Untouched by disease and fever, they spoke, as the plump Family man had preached, the plain language of the hills.

THE SPLIT HEART

Faisal outgrew the straw crib his mother fashioned, and the women of Maryam's sect built him a cot so that the child and mother slept with the acacia between them. As he fell asleep, Maryam recounted her pastoral childhood and in his flesh sketched with her fingernails the path from their shanty to the date field where she and her sisters harvested fruit and sold it to expectant women.

One night as the boy dozed, Maryam ran her hands through his starchy hair. His chest billowed hills and carved valleys. My aunt slipped on her sandals and stepped into the fog that had settled in the bowl of the valley. The peaks of the Family's tents poked through the clouds like fry bread in wheat porridge. A stray barked, but the night was troubled by no other jabberings.

Maryam ascended through patches of sprouting soy until she arrived at a plateau just below the crest. Then, as she had nearly every night for a month, my limber aunt summited the sandy hill. While perhaps not the cave of Hira, the high hill was Maryam's retreat, where she escaped the watchful ministrations of the women of the Family.

At other times, when she snuck into town, a veil drawn across her face, Maryam performed the promiscuous wanderings of an unkept woman. She stopped at the bookseller's stall.

Or smoked mint and tobacco from water pipes at the coffee-house, always fastidiously wiping the mouthpiece clean. Or at the ice seller's stall, she numbed her lips with an ill-gotten nugget, filched while the attendant tended an unruly goat.

Yet inevitably, a spry Familial, an oil-soaked rag around her face, found her and admonished my aunt for fleeing the sanctity of the encampment. She chaperoned Maryam's return, a firm hand on her elbow as if she were a wayward child.

Atop the hillock, Maryam could sit unmolested and survey the dust-hardened trail below. It was both the route by which the Family had fled the cursed town and the one she had once taken into Y_____ to meet her husband, leaving behind her younger sisters. Where they were now, she did not know. (She had written, but rarely receiving a reply, she had stopped.)

The trail led from Y_____, around the hillock, through a flat and featureless plain before plunging into a forest punctuated by stone hills that crouched in the inky night like bandits plotting an ambush. The fires of a caravan flickered deep in the forest.

From the pocket of her gown, Maryam fished a string of prayer beads. She worked them through her fingers and recited the Lord's many names. Thrice she prayed, before she wrapped the string around her palm, the green tassel tucked between her head and life lines.

Her head clearer and her own heart calmed, she returned to the tent where she confronted a pair of shadowy hulks, who seemed to hover above her sleeping son. The demons, or so she thought, addressed one another in a rapid tongue she could not decipher. But there was Faisal, sleeping soundly, and the menace needed no language for explanation.

Maryam raced at the men with her beads clenched in a raised fist. In a fluid motion as if rehearsing an intimate dance, one of the men caught her, put a warm hand over her mouth and swept her onto her cot. He placed his Jupiter finger against her lips. Heat spilled like an opiate from its point of contact, flush across her face, and crawled along her skin. Although she was awake, it was as if she could not remember where her muscles were or how they might be called into service. She could not think of what she might move. She could only stare and scowl at the men as they went about their mischief in the unlit tent.

Each scoundrel grasped an arm and lifted the sleeping boy into the air. With a swift tug and a sound like a tree sundered by an axe, the two cracked Faisal's chest down the center. The sight of it rent apart my aunt as if the child were still a growing part of her. A wail of horror rattled through her body like a boulder into a well.

As one of the men, if that's what they were, held the limp form of the boy aloft, the other took Faisal's beating heart from its pulpy home and tore it in half. From his robe, one of the iridescent men produced a gold basin packed with ice shavings. Perhaps, Maryam thought, they were sons of the ice seller. She envisaged her battalion of women stoning to death the cowering iceman and his brood with their own wintry blocks.

The men packed the cool shavings into the child's chest and rinsed his still-beating heart in the basin. With every contraction, the muscle spit an ochre slush. Once it had been thoroughly cleansed, the pair pressed the cleft heart back together, sealed it with the heat of their hands and placed it back into the boy's body.

My cousin slept through the whole grim procedure. His chest continued its unerring rise and fall, indifferent to its absent heart. The men danced their fingers across Faisal's chest, and his ribs snapped together like the iron latches of a gate.

As they left, one whispered in Maryam's ear, "Iblis touches every son of Adem the day his mother beareth him." My paralyzed aunt struggled with these words and their evocation of the beast. She struggled a final time against the toxin and then succumbed to its force.

When she awoke, my aunt knew of the men as a

nightmare—for the eye of the heart is open even in sleep. And yet, convinced that she had not been asleep, Maryam shredded Faisal's nightgown. My cousin startled awake and whimpered as his mother inspected every rib for a blemish or scar. She flipped the boy over and found no mark but the ones left long ago by the midwife. Not so much as a single lock of his girlish hair, that had yet to meet a scissors' clasp, seemed out of place.

Faisal stared at his mother as if she were consumed by mania. A flame passed through his pupils. But even then, he did not break his reticence, though he already had words to put on things.

When Maryam was satisfied he was unharmed, she pulled him close and enveloped him in her nightgown. The naked child sobbed into his mother.

My aunt never spoke to others of the strange visitation. As the midnight scorpions had been an augur to seal up her unborn, she took the ordeal as an omen. Her thoughts anticipated the trail, sallying out of town into the wilderness of the shadowed stones.

And so, Maryam quietly began to hoard supplies. As her husband's belongings had once cluttered the corners of her tent, they were slowly occupied by gourds of water, sachets of milk powder, lentils and tubers heaped in burlap and bolts of cloth that might mend garments. She packed no cases lest her warders grow suspicious and laid up her provisions in quilts instead. Years passed before her larder grew provocatively large and the women of the Family became more inquisitive. But a single question preyed upon my aunt: Where would she go?

One spring day, a courier arrived with a letter. Scripted across it: "Kansas Urchin Department."

Maryam held the brittle envelope, which had been worn velvety thin through much handling, and she read its contents: the sad story of her sister and her lame orphan nephew.

Finally, she thought, there is a place to go.

THE CHANGING SKIN

Maryam tucked the letter from the K.U.D. into her weathered pack. She rolled up the quilts that were stuffed with provisions, clothing, and lanterns. With a flat blade, she shaved her son's locks and dusted the clippings around the acacia.

Days before, she had seen a caravan flee Y_____. She waited until the fog returned before she set out for a new home with her boy, who was fast becoming a young man. Though she longed to visit the hillside slope where rested her daughter, my aunt knew that this foray was untenable as she feared waking Family members. Instead, as a remembrance of her life at Y_____, she carved bark from the acacia and plucked its fragrant flowers. Maryam placed them beside her husband's illustrated Holy Book and put the lot into her pack.

With the tents at the base of the knoll shrouded in thick mist, she packed into the bed of a wheelbarrow the bound quilts and a travel tent. She placed her bald son on top, as if bearing him on a palanquin. Faisal toyed with a corncob doll his mother had sewn. He took the ragged thing by its cloth arms and tugged. A crimson corn kernel popped from its chest, and he smiled.

Faisal bumped along atop the barrow as they stole out of their tent, descended the knoll, and wound through the camp, arousing mongrels, before they rounded the hillock out of sight. The moon, nearly full, hung low, and lit the trail. Because He is the One Who Guides, the Lord provided for Maryam and her son as He had for Hajar and Ismail.

Their path led into the forest, and my aunt lit a lantern. When it caught, she saw that a scorpion crouched ahead of her on the trail. Beset again, Maryam worried. She snatched the acacia bark from her pack and drove it into what she thought was the creature's hard middle. She swung the lantern but discovered only twigs and brush. Maryam exhaled, not realizing that she had been holding her breath, and spat out the acid that had built on her tongue. She tied tight the tails of her headscarf.

My aunt continued along the trail until she tired and her son slept. Dawn had broken, and the bilal's call swept across the forest. She read her prayers and pitched a tent. Their first day alone and together, Maryam slept curled around Faisal as the Family swept door-to-cowhide-flap-door through Y_____ and hunted for their missing matriarch.

During their journey from the outskirts of Y_____ to their residence in a mosque in eastern Kansas, Maryam and Faisal shadowed throngs of immigrants and refugees, remaining close enough to call for help should wolves or varmints have attacked, but otherwise sustaining themselves independently. At night, others hunched around fires and drank barley brew or smoked from long-handled pipes. They told one another of their lives to come as if these were real things, linens that could be worn and washed when soiled.

While the curses and the drunken laughter of the travelers punctuated the twilight, my aunt and cousin cocooned in their tent. At least, Maryam cooed to Faisal, this one didn't have a tree bursting through its center.

"When we wake every morning," she said as she kneaded oil into his calves, "there will be no thorns in our beds." Though she could smell them, she did not mention the sweet flowers that would fall from the acacia and perfume their cots.

She woke the next morning with dried petals in her hair and Faisal standing over her, bounding from foot to foot. To him she spoke the poet's words, "Smells are surer than sounds or sights, to make your heart strings crack."

But in migrants' tents, mothers worry. The journey to the Heartland took them from dispirited caravan to blighted town, from Tarshish to Quivira, from warring frontiers to serene plantations and across shallow streams and ceaseless seas, where in the rocking holds of ships mothers clutch their children to thwart the water's smothering embrace.

Toward the end of their hijra, my aunt and cousin encountered a caravan that had come to rest by a lake. The women led the children to a bank and began ablutions. After the boy rinsed, my aunt worked up the sleeves of her heavy gown and plunged her arms into the water. With a round of soap, she lathered herself. Above her elbows, she uncovered freckled patches that were as milky as soapstone. It was, she thought, as if her tea-colored skin had been pecked away.

Not knowing how far this Kansas was, Maryam anticipated a toll from the journey. Her barrow had splintered on a rock, so she bore Faisal on her back or found a spot for him on a passing oxcart when she could. At times Maryam glimpsed, she thought, the iridescent men who had mauled her son. But they vanished whenever she sought them.

The idea that she would be of a different skin by the time she reached her new home did not worry her. A new face, she thought, for a new life. Contrary to her wishes, the discoloration, which bound her to a son who had his own stain, did not rapidly spread. Instead, she slowly shed her shade. By the time they reached the Great Mosque of the Great State of Kansas, my aunt's face was a patchwork of olive-brown and milk-white. It gave her the painted look of a forlorn animal I had once slaughtered.

FELLING THE SON

Would that Maryam and Faisal had joined a wayward caravan and wandered the storied plains like members of a forsaken tribe. Would that my aunt and my cousin had consigned to oblivion the reason for their journey and found laughter in the Lord's decree! Would that that woman and that boy had found those false Kansans, the Arkansans, instead of us, and preached to them the habits of cleanliness and God-fearing-ness. Skills, I was told, they sorely lacked.

Though barn owls in the mosque delighted the worshippers, unlike my humble self the feebleminded masses didn't count scraping scat off the floors among their duties.

On the portentous morning that delivered my relations to our haven, in my distinguished post as Custodian and Caretaker of the Great Mosque of the Great State of Kansas I scratched my trowel against the tile and drowned out the imam's recitation. (He performed it in that ancient tongue, but it was a language from which I was sheltered: ignorance—my shield and my sword. The Lord be praised.)

But in the distance, thunder roared. Was it an early season whirlwind? My tower had been battered by one the year before, but the year before that there had been none. Was it a Missourian's mortar? You could trust, it seemed, only what you could see—ears too easily fooled by the mechanisms of machinery.

I sought the source of this added cacophony and pressed into the mosque's windows. From this vantage, I saw—no!—I bore witness to a low-hanging, fast-moving cloud as it swept alongside the weathered wall at the edge of our compound. My leg-irons chirped in nervous anticipation.

In past storms, we sheltered in the mosque's subterranean level, and the inclination to retire there gripped me. Why is the desire to flee so persistent in those who cannot do so with any artistry?

Commanded by the drover, the cattle cart broke from the cloud and chewed at the spring-softened trail. Canvas canopied the cart, and two, stout four-legged steers replaced the one five-legged one. Would that we could have bartered our relations as we did our livestock.

The menace advanced toward the mosque and scattered our goat herd, until the drover yanked the reigns. The cart halted at the men's entrance, but had they driven any further, they'd have been—*crash*—atop me.

A lone cloud seemed to hover above them.

From inside the mosque, I peered through a hole in the window delivered by a Missourian's ball. I jangled the copper pellets in the pocket of my tunic. Their clang was a salve for me like the bleat of a doe to its kids.

The drover shuffled in his tedious way to the cart's bed. I spied a substitute tobacco pouch in his denims. He presented a hand to a large veiled man and guided him to the ground. He kissed this gentleman's hand as if he were the Grand Mufti of our State, and then the drover retrieved quilts and a possibles bag and deposited them outside the mosque. With a "hup hup," he returned to his seat and retreated with his wagon. But the cloud remained and shaded this mysterious mufti.

Who was this sir? I wondered. I could not recall a chivalry ever performed by the micturating drover. Prayer time was also not near. And where had I left the footbath? The Dignitary's soap? The trowel slipped from my grasp and clanked to the floor. My hand pressed into an oily palm print deposited on the window by a parishioner.

The veiled man strode through the men's archway and brushed aside a pair of brown leathers that had drifted away from the other shoes. And that is when I discovered that this gentleman was not one. As she entered the mosque, this gentlewoman's shadow spilled across the tile and came to rest between my defective feet.

I had never seen a woman so big that she could block out the sun. I inhaled and nudged myself backwards.

She seemed to sequester light. All the windows in Topeka were no match for her darkening presence. She walled the men's entrance with her absurd carriage, and had any hefty miners arrived they would have struggled to pass by.

Her stature ridiculed our Kansan women—underfed creatures who asserted their physical primacy only when with child. I had difficulty in those days telling the boys from the women, their frames and statures, the loping that passed for walking. The slovenliness that passed for personhood. I assumed everyone was a man. Girls were men; women were men; horses were men too.

But there are things, I have learned, that even horses should not do. These included walking into the mosque through the men's entrance.

This woman was an example of how a woman could be, could occupy a man's space, something to provide shade in the middle western heat, a woman-husk to stuff with other women, other men. In the days after her arrival, she would make us wonder if we truly weren't men, but women whose faces hadn't yet lost their beards. As a citizenry, she gave us hope that a future State could be peopled with women like her, men like her too.

With each step, the matron's coarse gown seemed to yield more fabric as if a team of diligent sewers worked quickly to cover her. I thought I saw a hand of one of these attendants flatten a crease. A lace headscarf obscured her face, but her chin, which jutted out, had a patchwork, a mottled appearance.

She glided to me, veiled me in her shadow. Did I hear a hound call?

From behind her, an orb spun off—a young man seemed to cough out the fabric, as if the team who mended her dress pushed him through a fold, then stitched it to regain an illusion of wholeness.

He was not introduced to me as my cousin Faisal, our Savior. Nor was the woman introduced as my aunt. No bells chimed. No trumpets blared. Drums remained unstruck. I remember the near quiet and Bahira's wavering voice. Tea simmered. An owl swept from the dome and speared an intrepid varmint.

It was clear that the pair was related: He was just an unveiled, diminutive version of his mother. And this fellow was like me—not a boy but not quite a man. But I was larger than him, older by a dimension. His hands would have fit into mine had we played such games. His hair, a charcoal color, formed a tight bowl not unlike mine, I marveled. He had wide eyes, a sonorous brown, if colors can be said to produce sounds, and lighter than my own. A nascent beard feathered onto his cheeks. His cloak was funereal, a muddy eggshell color. He carried a fanged scent, if odors can be said to have teeth. I have come to associate this scent with transients, doused as they were by the Kansas Welcoming Committee, which greeted and deloused refugees.

His skin, the murkiness of chicory coffee, was shades darker than mine—as if, where he had come from, the sun wasn't a thing from which you should cower. He would learn. This was Kansas. Our grass withered in the fields. Our heat, our sun was punishing. That was why we knew there was a Lord, the Eternal Owner of Sovereignty. That was why our chirrs grew fatter off our land than did our people.

There was also something difficult about his face. As others have noted in the verse commissioned upon his expiration, which I shall not afflict upon you, his face seemed to float from his meat and project ahead of him. It glimmered or smoldered—I'm not sure which is correct. I will leave that to the poets.

This young man and his mother, now the very symbols of our blessed State, were upon their arrival the anti-Kansans. She was imposing, eclipsing. He, merely a cast-off river stone. From what I had seen, they belonged in the State Fair, anchoring the Great Freaks of the Great State: See Little Man and Big Momma!

These new arrivals, these immigrants from a land I would not know. They smelled their caustic smell. They replaced what we had known. They worshipped in their way—familiar, yes, but also unfamiliar.

This fellow's artless eyes sought his mother's cloaked face before they found my leg-irons. He cheated around her to gaze on my skewed legs, beseeching them to divulge the geometry of my deformity

Disgorged from his mother's fabric, the young man and his questioning face approached me. My leg braces reflected him as in a carnival mirror, a hideous, elongated thing, and I decided that I didn't need his anti-Kansan questioning. So, I acted on instinct as is my wont and thrust a part of my body, my mouth, in his direction to assault him with maledictions. But the words caught in my throat and failed to disable him. So much for conducting mouth wars.

My hands found my pockets, and I launched the pellets at his face. The Lord be praised.

A direct hit caused his eyes to roll back and he to syrup to the floor. He snatched for his mother's cloth, his fingers snapping like a pond turtle.

Rain came by way of the copper pellets, and mosque birds swept in to hunt the rattling feed. The Incident of the Pellets, as it would be known, remained the only time, I assure you, that I struck out in such a manner. And it should be understood why I forswore the collection of such ammunition again.

The matron wiped his tears with the sleeve of her gown. She then clasped me by the shoulders and hoisted me up, pressing herself into me. My irons dangled at the end of my legs, and I searched with my face but could feel no other women in her garment. The fabric corseted me as if I would become part of her, a substitute child for the ones who had escaped.

She cooed, "there there, now." It was comfort dropped from a high place. "The Lord guides who He chooses," she offered. She seemed to reprimand me for wounding her son by offering succor—a form of sanction to which I was unaccustomed. I hung in her arms, absorbed her rich fields, buried in her dress, embraced by the woman who with her son would inspire our new Country, our Vatican on the Plains.

It was, I suppose, not lost on her that this was the first time she was meeting her urchin nephew. The product of her lost sister and husband. My mother, my father. But was I told that I had relations? That relations were to be arriving? I was not.

Then, the woman raised me even higher. She peered into my eyes with hers and searched, it seems clear to me now, for an affirmation of familial physiognomy. If she found one, I was not told. For at that same time, the imam emerged from his office with a vial of rosewater in one hand and a chunk of flatbread in the other. Crumbs studded his beard.

I slipped from the women's clutches and clunked to the floor as gracefully as I could, while the leviathans exchanged welcomes in that ancient tongue. The imam clucked as the lady unfurled herself. She was nearly his size. My legs chirped away, and a whimper escaped from the fellow on the floor.

"Bahira?" she asked, using his given name as if they had

been familiar. He affirmed and called out to her, "Maryam?" She assented. It was a first jig in a courtship that would find for this woman and her son, and to my dismay, a partnership.

From her pack, the lady unveiled a letter with those familiar initials, K.U.D., and released it to the imam. Was I transferred along with its contents?

Bahira held the letter and my aunt's patchwork hands before reading the disquiet on her face, deposited by my sedition. He regarded the young man on the tile and the copper pellets that were scattered around. Bahira's beard registered its dyspepsia.

"Would you? You would use the tools of the Missourians against your own people?" he bellowed in what was certainly a preening display for the new arrivals. He hoisted me by an ear like festering trash, as if clumps of bread stuck in my beard. As if I were blocking out the sun. As if I were on the floor blubbering.

The imam then discharged me and attended to the lad. He garlanded him with his prayer beads. There were times, I thought, that sons inherited their father's pistols. But for the chicken-hearted like the imam, perhaps a necklace sufficed.

In an attempt, I believed, to redeem my contemptible and loathsome presence, the preacher slammed the bottle of rosewater into my hand and instructed me to employ it on our guests. I dabbed some in my palm, the scent as cloying and noxious as ever, and sprinkled it in the neighborhood of the lady.

I dashed the rest of the bottle onto the young man as if I pissed rosewater. It seemed fitting that he should receive no less the welcome that I had, and I was certain the ambrosia refreshed his travel-weary hide.

The preacher hoisted me once again by my ear. A freshly denuded switch rested against the minaret should he have chosen to employ it on my womanly skin, but instead he carted me up the 100-odd steps of my tower in his awkward crouch and deposited me on the straw bed. He glowered, stroked his face and showered down crumbs. His beard flashed silver, before it returned to a muddy brown. My counterfeit father stormed away, and I heard the latch on the door fart shut as he sealed me in. My ear hurt in my head. My head hurt from my head too.

I inventoried my room: whitewashed walls, a suitcase, stacks of threadbare scriptures, a clutch of tools, a keg of powder. The meager belongings of a tenuous presence. A crack had formed at the base of the wall near the window. The time for fruit bats had yet to come. I unfastened my leg braces and placed them in the case with a spare tunic. I lay in my nest, my head on a pillow stuffed with the imam's torn clothes. They reeked of his soured scent.

After the unpleasantries at our introduction, the matron took the imam's direction in deciding when and how to address my woeful form. And after the earlier incidents with the horse and with the Fanatics, the imam addressed me only to confirm or assign custodial duties or to place blame on those tasks that had escaped my sloth. As if his words would nourish me.

The lady told me that she forgave me for assaulting her son, but I suspected that she did not. To wit: Was I offered cream from her healing bosom to assuage my deformity? I was not. Though at the time, I did not even know there was such a salve to be offered!

Perhaps because the imam wanted to sequester her from other possible suitors, the woman and the young man were given the mosque's subterranean level in which to reside, which resulted in the displacement of my custodial instruments! But when she was finished with it, you would not have thought it the modest dwelling of a diviner's wife had you seen the shine she conjured from those disagreeable grounds. Perhaps she was appreciative of our strong edifices after wintering in transient shelters, or perhaps she simply had an aptitude for homemaking that rivaled her storytelling ability!

Predictably, the imam arranged a festivity in her and the lad's honor. It was during this event that I came to learn of our relations. Before the assembled masses, from a sunflower festooned dais the preacher gestured in my direction and informed all that the "malformed urchin" was the nephew of "the most gracious travelers" who were now "filling the mosque and our community with a joy, a joy and a hope, that could only spring from the devotion of those who had known true hardship. For is He not also the Infuser of Faith!" I cannot remember such revelry inflicting our ummah again until the loathsome and trying day of my cousin's marriage to Ms. A_____!

But was I happy? I had, courtesy of the imam and hardships faced by this woman and her son, received the blessing of a family. And wasn't that what all malformed urchins desired? A people to whom they belonged? For does not the Lord say: *Did He not find you an orphan and give you refuge?*

But happiness was not an emotion I had husbanded. In truth, I did not know that I should have felt it at the imam's revelation, and so I did not. And that lack of feeling, that presence of unfeeling, was what in me persisted. It was what I husbanded, what I nurtured and what I nurture still.

After the imam's proclamation, Faisal and I joined the priest at the front of the prayer hall. He held two pieces of rope, which Bahira first tied to his hands and then to ours.

"This covenant, this—this twine," he stammered, "signifies your allegiance to the Lord and to our Prophet, who is ours and who is a Prophet of the Lord."

"Amen," I whispered first. Then my aunt singed the rope, and we were released. And like that, my cousin and I passed into official man-hood. We shook hands and then hugged, though I had to fight the urge to smother him in my embrace. As I have said, I was merciful.

When the festivities died down, my aunt asked me to

accept my menial role in life. "Son," she advised, "it is not up to us how the Lord has chosen to make us."

To which I replied: "Would that it was." The Lord be praised.

As Auntie Maryam had once found her son a berth on a cattle cart, the imam offered Faisal a prized seat at his side. My cousin wrapped the priest's prayer beads around his hand or draped them on his neck.

I, on the other hand, clanked along. Per usual.

THE SERPENT AND THE DOME

The arrival of my relations prompted the physical transformation of not only the subterranean floor of our mosque, but of the entire place itself! The disrepair, which harbored us for a sick hound's lifetime, suddenly required mending. Mending that was discharged by my meager hands!

Instructed by our preacher, I executed the tasks: patching the outhouse, re-boring the lines from the cistern to the taps, clearing rubble from the scorched yard. If I expected assistance from my treasured cousin, I found none. While I labored, he and the imam whittled meat together in the morning, sauntered through the acreage in cordial contemplation, and perused holy books and histories of our storied people.

Did he learn that old tongue? That old script? He did, and his recitation quavered from the preacher's office until he gained the vocation of a bilal. In my modest manner, I would press myself to the sealed door of the office to pry. Like Faisal's faces, his verse propelled into you, branded itself on your chest. It was a skill, learned I assumed, that augured future rhetorical triumphs.

As the First Winter threatened to descend, Bahira proclaimed that the dome over the prayer hall must be tarred and sealed. And so, ladders arrived by way of the drover. None of them, however, proved of enough height for us to scale the holy house, and my attempts at banding the rungs together culminated in a near calamity that would have found my precious head re-bandaged!

The imam consulted with his prized disciple, my cousin, and their mental hardship resulted in the architecting of a hoist device. One not dissimilar, it should be noted, to the hook-and-rope apparatus I employed in the shed with the slaughter goats. Their device featured a pulley and scaffold, but in principle operated in the same manner: The sacrifice was in this case harnessed, not trussed, and then raised to a favorable position.

After days of construction, the time came to test the hoist. I chose the noble weakling, assured that even if the ridiculous contraption failed, we would be guaranteed goat meat without risking a more robust animal. Was I thanked for this foresight? I was not.

The test they held after the midday congregational prayer for what reason I did not know. Had it failed before the worshippers would they have faulted my cousin? The imam? My aunt?

In any case, it did not fail.

At first.

I harnessed the beast and patted its bewildered head, *there there now,* and then my cousin and the imam hoisted, demonstrating that they could exert themselves if sufficiently provoked. Once the animal was raised, the contraption swung and deposited the goat atop the mosque. Cheers of "God-is-Great" erupted, and save for me and the suspended creature, enthusiasms and devotions were declared. With the animal still harnessed, the process was reversed. The goat skittered away after I unleashed it. In fact, I cannot remember seeing it again.

The next day when morning prayers concluded, which were led by my cousin for I believe the first time, the confederate pair set about hoisting my precarious form atop the dome. I collected my implements and a bucket of fastening tar I had been heating on a campfire and placed them on a pallet. It was to be hoisted up after me—that was the initial plan. I slipped between the ropes, and the boy and the preacher heaved.

Once airborne, the harness strangled the sparrow between my legs. Before I could protest, I was atop the mosque and once again on my feet.

The ease at my elevation was quickly betrayed by the adversity incurred when I landed: I spooked a copperhead who had been sunning himself in a luxurious, undisturbed manner. A manner that I envied.

The snake was of significant and unavoidable heft, and through the deployment of fanged atrocities made clear his displeasure at my intrusion. I was, as you are aware, unafraid of combat, but without a shovel or blade with which to dispatch the occupier, I re-harnessed and quickly dove off the roof.

But my pace carried me farther than the slipshod hoist could accommodate!

In a half circle, I swung above my cousin and the imam. A loud crack then jolted me, and then I dropped. At that moment, a prayer may have escaped my lips. Or a deluge of maledictions. But instead of plummeting to my uncertain demise, in this suspended position I remained.

From what I could see, a bracket had snapped in the lever arm and then engaged with the splintered wood of the hoist. Or some such geometry. As I have said I was not a scholar—just an accomplished pupil.

The boy's and preacher's efforts to disengage the hoist proved fruitless and in truth, were rather amusing—were I not the one condemned by their lack of ability. I did not make known my displeasure overtly, but instead acted as if this inconvenience were another of the routine insults that beset me, which was an honest summary even though I was greatly displeasured and discomforted.

I enlightened the milling rabble on the snake's infestation of the mosque's dome, to which they responded with alarm and concern far exceeding that which they had manifested for my dangling form. As I floated above like an irregular, un-iridescent angel, the imam and my cousin interrogated me on the copperhead's color, temperament and so on. As if its presence alone weren't reason enough for misgivings and the judicious deployment of a blade.

They returned to the mosque to confer with my aunt as I swung on counterfeit gallows. A bomb burst nearby, kindling for a moment the crooked crescent that dangled from the dome. Would that I had had a smoke to aide in the passing of my suspended time!

My curious form delighted passersby and worshippers. Was I, they questioned, exhibiting a new mechanism of devotion? Of penance? They could not discern which, such was their retrograde aptitude. Sympathy from them at my pathetic lot would have been, of course, impertinent. Several derelict cadets, unregenerate boys no doubt expelled from the mosque by a humorless disciple of the imam's, hurled stones or insults: And thus, the names Scrub Brush, Scrub Tree or simply Scrub or Brush adhered to my person. As if my given name would have no purchase in their imaginations.

After daylight and my appendages withered, the drover returned. By lamplight, he and others fashioned a ladder and platform to liberate me from my festering perch. My legs had atrophied from their strangulation by the rope harness, and to convalesce I was deposited atop prayer rugs inside the mosque. Also, I was given meat porridge by my aunt. I will admit that the sublimity of her broth, its alchemistry, was a welcome betterment to the porridge which I forged and to which I had grown accustomed. She was, let it not go unsaid, adept at these culinary and domiciliary assignments. But I failed to discern the quality in her that made the poets crow. Maryam of the Milk she may have been, but like the townsfolk of Y_____, I could not see it.

It was from this supine position that I overheard the preacher, my cousin, and their companions opining on the snake. That boy, schooled as he was in the old texts that were not made available to my canny person, recalled a tale: The Cube, he affirmed, had been beset as well! And the Lord had eradicated the infestation in due time. For is He not also the One who Relieves.

For me, this confirmed only that our progenitors inhabited as feral and beset a Country as we did. But the compatriots and disciples saluted my cousin with fawning and appreciative declarations: "You are a sayer of truth," one declared! "A doer of good," another added!

They all concluded that, "Like the Cube, our holy house should not be altered or modified"—that the sanctity of the sanctuary was not to be perturbed.

While the outcome of their deliberation would delay for me the unpleasant tarring and fastening of the dome, I thought it gibbering insanity. Rain, snow, varmints, Missourians—we were routinely molested! A point I would have raised had it not already been decided that until the serpent departed, no further rehabilitation of the mosque was to commence.

But for my meager person, toil was ever present. With the hoist contraption repaired, a process commenced every morning after prayers led by my cousin in an increasingly honed and some might say bewitching tongue (if we were the types to believe in witches, which we were not) wherein I was again harnessed and raised to assess the snake and its disposition.

And each day I encountered the menace exposing its horrors. Although I believed I could have assisted with the snake's dispatching as I had become adept with the goat knife, I was instructed to leave it, "As long as the praiseworthy Lord has decided it shall rest."

Instead, I plotted: Could I operate the hoist and elevate myself in the moonless night? I could ambush the serpent

and wear its pelt in triumphant celebration like those sons of
Adem. Then would my name have had purchase in the imagination of our peoples!

But I could not both leverage the hoist and propel myself
atop the mosque. The contraption required at least two toilers,
and a cripple and a goat pressed into service were poor surrogates.

On the seventh or ninth day after the proclamation, I forget
which, as I was harnessed, a tufted hawk—perhaps the same one
who had assaulted the imam the day I arrived—swooped in and
snatched the squirming copperhead to fly away I did not know
where. And with the bird's assistance, my work repairing the
dome resumed. The Lord had removed, all concluded, the threat.

When it came time to replace the bronze crescent that
crowned our mosque, tar-covered I assisted the imam as we
hoisted my cousin into glorious position atop the dome. The scaf-
folding held, and worshippers cheered. May the Lord be praised.

Faisal's prescience aided his and his mother's notoriety—
as if prognosticating that a hawk would devour a snake was
the equivalent of cleaving a moon apart and raising a sacred
mountain between the gleaming halves. Soothsayers are
given wide berths by their credulous disciples and, as I have
mentioned, we Kansans were in wanting times. Would that
we could divine the Lord's intentions without the need for
sweet-sermoning siblings.

To compound my cousin's purported divinity, Bahira, if I
may be familiar, bellowed when he uncovered the blemish he had
been seeking since at least my arrival. What had him convinced
that smears between the brittle blades of my cousin's shoulders
amounted to the imprint of divinity, I was unsure. A feast of my
knowledge, it should not be forgotten, would starve a vole.

Certainly, citizenry of every bearing found themselves scarred
and stained by innumerable fists and calamities—and may the

Lord safeguard us if each one of them declares themselves a Negus or Prophet! Did my double deformities anoint me? No, they did not, but of my cousin's sanctity the imam did seem convinced. And his conviction, like sloth, was infectious in our land.

And so, the sermons began.

And they did begin tepidly. You have heard from those dramatists, lyricists, and balladists on the artistry of my cousin's sermonizing. Would that our poets were as skilled in the study of texts as they are fond of creating them! Faisal's Prophet's Day teachings were reformulations of Holy Book verses delivered in an earlier untamed murmur by the imam!

Was I not present for the very first of the Sayings?

I was.

Faisal ascended that gleaming minbar, which I had refurbished with red oak, and began preaching: *"The Garden of Immortality is promised to the pious."*

You would think that a plainspoken and tattered truism would find no audience to court. And yet, this phrase was all I was able to heed before a herd of worshippers pummeled past me to crowd around my cousin. And as has happened several times during my regrettable residence, I found myself spat from the mosque like the pits of a prairie apple. (And like those seeds, I too have proliferated. I too have fathered.)

Yes, the Garden of Immortality: The graveyard in which we buried my cousin was named for his first sermon. I can see it now, his tomb, from my prison perch. How lonely he looks. I shall not join him there, but I did liberate him. I did inter him. Discharged by my meager hands.

In the days after the First Sermon but before the arrival of the Family of Parts and with them my beloved, the reverence paid to our pastoral premises would have confounded any astute observer: Citizenry beset us! Prayer or not, they shuffled into our compound as if simple proximity to my cousin and his mother would becalm the djinns that tormented them.

My aunt and the imam corralled the hordes and distributed the tributes that had amassed. My crafty cousin escaped from the worshipful, however. Regretfully, his escape was the very place I inhabited and in which I am now entombed!

I had by then been subsisting with a facility in my tower. I even considered it mine as, save for the few occasions on which the imam inspected—a switch of menacing willow in hand, no one else had entered the circle room atop the minaret. Was my harvest any greater? Of course: Innumerable horns, antlers, molars salvaged from departed beasts jangled in my cloister. The unexecuted powder keg swathed like a suckling babe.

One day as I conjured the image of a covered woman uncovered save for an antler neckpiece, an image that I exploited with which to pleasure myself, I heeded faint footsteps on the stone. Their cadence was muffled, as if a woman other than my aunt were approaching. These were not the heavy bearded thumpings of the imam's footsteps, of that I was certain.

A knock rattled the metal portal, and I sheathed my songless sparrow. It was the boy, my cousin. Escape, he bleated, he needed. I allowed him audience, and because as I have said I was sociable, I swept a wilted arm across my empire. He reclined on my mattress. A satchel of coarse rocks, the ones I employed to spook our worshippers, rested beside the bed. Faisal worked a handful in his palm.

I had seldom heard my cousin complain, but a weariness creased his callow and increasingly bearded face, which for the moment had shed its glimmer or smolder. "The Lord's words," he bemoaned, "shed more ink than all the seas. When I sleep, dawn breaks beneath my eyes." He pressed his hands into his face as if to shutter the glow that besieged him as it once had his mother.

Was I to help him? Provide a sympathetic shoulder on which he should lay his weariness? A sip of tobacco?

In any case, I did not, and he sprawled across my mattress, nonetheless.

It is hard for me to describe what next occurred—I was not a scholar nor was I a dramatist, as I have noted. This much I know: I was unsure what I saw. His clay, from a reclining position, seemed to propel itself upwards as if the hands that had once corralled his mother's wayward garments levitated him from my nest.

I snatched my quilts to subdue him in case he took flight. As I have said, I was considerate.

Floating, it seemed, above the straw mat, Faisal sat upright, scattering the stones. He washed his hands across his face and chest in the manner of a housecat or tidy varmint. Then, he held out his palms as if in prayer. My lantern flickered as a bomb scared whitewash from the tender walls, but our Savior did not recoil. The glimmer of his face returned, and Faisal asked that I leave. His voice staggered as if a thing obstructed his throat.

As I departed, I sealed the portal. Perhaps the castings squealed in a manner that parodied the palaver of our day or perhaps I heard someone say, "Peace, O Messenger." And I scraped down the stairs.

I found succor in the foyer of my tower and slumbered atop a quilt until the sun broke through the keyholes. At some point during the gloom, the boy forsook my chambers for when I returned upstairs to collect my implements, he was unpresent. In his stead, a mound of polished stones gleamed on the mattress. It did seem like a fair barter—the stones for my cousin—as are all the Lord's arrangements

After this first visit, my cousin took refuge in *my* chambers! Between prayers as I shuffled from chore to ceaseless chore, he found solace in my cloister, which became his personal Hira if that noble cave had an attending mother who deposited a pewter tray with porridge at the minaret's stable door.

I would count the rations as my own if they had gone unconsumed by the evening prayer.

THE GOAT'S BLADDER

As I have said, my toil began with daybreak and concluded with the worship that followed the setting of the rust-colored sun. Although I had taken a strong dislike to these ministrations due to the difficulties that beset me, I often malingered at the rear of the prayer hall with my head bowed and my arms at my side, knocked about by parishioners as they rose and kneeled and jerked themselves, communing with the Lord-Seated-in-Heaven as Faisal led us, sermon by sermon, prayer by prayer, to the Garden of Immortality—not to the graveyard but to Paradise.

Auntie Maryam accompanied the imam in deed if not in name. They conferred in his office, reciting verse and repeating the Lord's name, bellying-bumping for all I knew! When I could, with the mosque unblemished, the cistern full and the chamber pots gleaming, I pressed myself to the sealed doorway as if it would reveal the secrets that passed inside. The wood beguiled whatever stiff messages I was meant not to hear. Once again impeded by nature.

And on an otherwise trivial day, I bore witness to an occurrence now anointed in our Histories: Like the babe Ismail who struck his heel and summoned a spring in the uncultivated valley, so too did Faisal liberate our people from those Kawsmouth-occupying villains!

That summer had scorched our Country. The chirrs devoured our crops, and it was made doubly worse as it coincided with the Fasting Month. Oh, those long days! The war for the Kaw fared poorly. Eastern rivers had been overcome, and rumors abounded of Bushwhackers damning the Kansas River as well. You cannot say that we do not live among the imaginative.

The drover proved himself a chicken-heart by refusing to trek to the waters. He claimed an alleged incident during which he'd escaped a band of terrorists by ditching the deadweight, life-preserving water barrels. I was unpresent for that harvest: Would that the drover had ended up wrapped in muslin in the bed of his own cart! I would have drove that cart to somewhere far-off and hospitable like beautiful, bountiful Colorado!

We went unwatered until my cousin, no doubt deploying his lyrical dexterity, persuaded that squirrel-faced man to harvest from a lake far northwest of our habitations, near our border with those comically misshapen Nebraskans. (Have you seen a sketch of one? You cannot help but laugh at the malformation that passes for a Nebraskan noggin! One of the Lord's ninety-nine names is not The Japer, but I remain convinced that He is one!)

Our customs, which exhorted routine ablutions because we apparently soiled ourselves with great ease and frequency, were made mockery during those parched days when we were forced to scrub ourselves with chalk, like those beasts I have not grown fond of. When washing, powdered limestone was a poor substitute for river water! Also, you could not make tea or coffee with it. But the does were gravid—for is not one of the Lord's names The Provider? And their milk and the meat of their offspring sustained us.

Nevertheless, the Histories is as such: My cousin and his feather-bearded disciples filed out of the prayer hall. He and these graduated tenderfoots, inducted by the hearth, had taken to calling themselves the Society of the Brothers of the Imam,

which was meant to signify fealty to certain Mahometan ideals
but would for me represent only consternation and dread. At
the close of each week's Prophet's Day sermon, the imam met
with the Brothers and recounted tales of our people when we
belonged not to the plains but to the widowed desert, if such a
thing could be imagined!

The confederates passed by me as I whetted my blade. Did
the Fanatic's gore still stain the walls? It did but was faded by
my hands and also by the thousand fingers of the sun.

My cousin hefted a chicken axe, the sort I employed on the
slim hindquarters of a goat, and I scuffed behind the beadles
as they wound through a thicket into the forest. Faisal slashed
a pair of oak limbs, handed them to a Brother, who stripped
clean the branches. Had they inquired, I could have stripped
them, but I was not then—nor am I now—a Brother.

The crowing of cicadas choked the shouts of the boys. For
this I was thankful.

We clamored out of the forest into the field behind the
mosque, which thanks to my labors had been cleared of debris
and wreckage. Thunder cracked. Miners not Missourians. The
Lord be praised!

The disciples shooed a flock that snacked on the rancid,
imam-seeded goat-meat, and a Brother carved a circle into the
dust in an inelegant way. They commenced a game: Each took
a turn inside the circle and attempted with a stick to strike
another stick that was lobbed to him. Faisal struck well, though
I suspected that the others pitched more charitably to him—
the vigor of diviners' sons notwithstanding.

The pack of goats rambled across the ground—the regal
offspring of my departed friend. The soft tumble of their
excrement trailed behind them. The Brothers threw stones,
chased them away. Was there a more satisfying sound than
that of stone striking hollow chest?

Although the dayslamp had found its western home,

sunlight persevered. I watched as Auntie Maryam emerged from her habitations on the ground floor of our holy house. (Why a cripple boy was not offered these chambers in which to reside, which would have been a far shorter descent from the prayer hall than was the ascent into the room atop the minaret, was one of many oversights regarding my care and habitation. Oversights that have had unfortunate consequences. Rather than descend 100-odd stairs on rickety legs to answer nature's most glorious call, I had found it my liking to emanate from my window. Was I to know that on a particular day the drover would be delivering grain for the mosque? No, I did not know, and so I befouled him and the foodstuffs! And once befouled, the squirrel-faced man ratted me out as if he himself had not befouled me once upon a time! In turn, the imam handed him a limb of stripped willow like an olive branch or an offering. I can tell you that from years of beast-lashing, that drover had developed a zealous arm. After my flagellation, I was delegated cloth diapers. For freeing me of their bondage, I should thank you, Faisal.)

To escape my aunt's gravity, I retired to the minaret where I batted about a goat bladder pouch that I had stitched together. From my perch, I saw swarms of lightning bugs shimmering around the mosque. True, they were a nuisance to our garden, but at least they held some charming spectacle, unlike many relations I knew. The Brothers snatched the critters from their dance and stuffed them into jars, creating makeshift lanterns so that they could continue jousting into nightfall.

But soon the chill came, and the runts' parents quit their worship and called out to their brood. When the last Brother had quit, I returned to the pitch where Faisal disgorged the bugs from the lanterns. I scrambled to the circle and hoisted the striker, tossing the goat-pouch into the vault before swinging. But the bladder thudded to the dust. A gust spit dirt in my eye, and I may have teared.

Though I was often defeated, in the twilight I persisted.

The very next time I tossed the pouch, I cracked it good and long—across the field and outside the lamplight. Even that cousin boy did not hide his glee, which he demonstrated by trying to sequester the striker away from me! He swung a bug lantern at me, and its fire rippled in his eyes!

Undeterred, I scurried to the bladder, tossed it up again, and connected with a smack—the pouch sailing right above Faisal's beloved head. Would that I had had more victories in this churlish world. The Lord be praised.

But to my surprise, Faisal seemed pleased by my display, and we raced back-and-forth across the field, smacking the bladder, until out of breath, I collapsed in the chill onto the barren earth.

I had in my meager way outrun myself, and I cried for water, clutching my chest, heaving and rolling like a submissive hound.

Faisal straddled me as if I were a vanquished foe. He snatched the striker and slapped my flank. As if he were the first to use nature against me in this manner. The imam's beads rattled against his chest, though they did not produce a rich tone.

I have never regretted an action of mine or rather I have always regretted actions of mine, but in any case, I glared into the dizzying vault as my thoughts drifted to the copper pellets, the smoothed stones.

"You move swiftly in those," Faisal proclaimed, tapping my leg iron.

I sputtered. A salvo of coughs thieved my breath.

Faisal appeared unconcerned with my frail state and scanned for the bladder pouch.

"Water," I pleaded and motioned for him to return to the mosque. The sky began to scumble, and an angry weather formed in my chest.

His eyes extinguished for the moment, Faisal filliped the bladder, captivated by it like string to a crow. He then made for the mosque but stopped suddenly, grasping the striker with both hands, bringing it up to his chest. Faisal drove the wood like a stake into the bladder, undoing my handiwork as the pouch popped and wheezed.

But in doing so, the Plains Prophet cracked an ancient reservoir, because from where he struck, a geyser sprung, drenching us both.

The vault thundered again as flares went up. Missourians not miners.

We stared at the curious spring before my cousin tossed the striker into the brush and unto me said, "Here is your water. Drink, friend." Faisal then dried himself with his embroidered tunic and wrung dry his knit cap.

I lapped up what I could. The drink calmed the heaves but filled my mouth with a wet silt that I coughed back up. Overtaken by the rush of water, "Stop," I pleaded with the spout, "Stop!" A fruit bat landed beside me and slithered its tongue into the stream.

Would that our tales were as plentiful as those who tell them!

Word spread from Faisal's glorious face to his mother's and to the imam's. And sooner than I cared to admit—did not our Country take a fortnight to cross by camel?—it seemed that all of Kansas arrived to catch a glimpse of my cousin, the Magician. That I had been the one to show him the game that sprung the ceaseless spring was lost between the storytellers and the told.

I had found ministering to the mosque tedious when it brimmed with partisans. When the rest of our State arrived, the sanctuary guttered with work. Auntie Maryam oversaw the construction of a well on the site of my cousin's "hallowed divinations," or so said our Governor on his first visit. (On his second, after our defeat of the Missourians at the Ditch, he would resign his post. Then with the imam and my cousin at his side, he would recite the Holy Book.)

After morning prayers, teams of parishioners hefted wheat-colored stones to the well-works. They set up a campsite nearby, so the work could proceed from one morning's prayer to the next. The laborers, men with grit in their gums, affixed the cross-beams atop the well and a phalanx of buckets to the windlass. The families of these men tended the campsite, and when they broke for lunch or worship, the men sailed their shrieking children through the sky.

Though without a family of my own, I joined the laborers, wiping my brow on my tunic as I filled barrows with stones and guided them straight and true to the site. My aunt, sipping tea, surveyed from the mosque. The ends of her ashen gown trailed into the dust.

It should come as no surprise when I reveal to you that the imam and that cousin were seldom seen during the well's construction. Instead, they met with various other clerics and dignitaries from adjacent counties—the youngest Brothers washing the feet of these weary travelers, not I.

Construction of the "Stop, Stop" well proceeded from the crescent to the full moon. Miners from a nearby quarry uncovered a slab of obsidian, which the imam proclaimed was fallen from the Heavens—as if he were a qualified judge. A contingent led by Faisal inspected the divine rock and anointed it with healing and cleansing powers as if we were the disciples of a stone-worshipping clan, which we were not.

The hallowed hunk found its way into my barrow. And it did captivate my relentless attention. The stone was not impoverished: It had the heft of a horse's head. When the light caught it, like the imam's beard it transformed into a muddy amber. I traced my fingers across its scarred surface but felt none of these so-called powers lest they worked on man in a muted manner.

Faisal would lay this holy stone as the final step in the well's construction: Under a cloudless sky, the field behind our mosque teemed with worshippers, miners, Kansans. The wind bullied bonnets from the heads of babes while the sun gleamed from its exulted perch. Perhaps the chirrs did not chirp. With Faisal and my aunt beside him, the imam circled the well and recited verses in that ancient tongue. Citizens of every ilk echoed the outsized man in word and deed. I looked above, where else would you look? A flock of insidious crows mimicked the partisans in their circuit around the well. Even the animals, it seemed to me, revered the procession.

The imam motioned for me, and I drove the inky block to my cousin. For the occasion, Faisal dressed in a silk tunic, which was obtained by his mother from a generous and devout trader. I patted down my own blood-stained garments.

With the imam's assistance, my cousin hoisted the obsidian into a gap in the well-wall. Then using my trowel, he slapped on mortar in an ill-suiting manner. It was clear that unlike me, he had little practice in masonry. Faisal held the instrument aloft, and a cheer—God is Great!—ripped through the crowd. May the Lord be praised.

Faisal was then to regale the assembly with the Story of the Well, at least that was the initial plan, when a motley hoard, who you will remember as the so-called Family of Parts, reeking of astringent, elbowed their way to the front, eliciting rebukes from our citizenry.

A man so rotund that he could have been called Kansan stumbled up to my aunt. The imam obstructed the man's path with his surly frame, his beard reddening.

"We have been searching for you, Maryam," the man exclaimed, pressing past our spiritual leader. "Now we have found you!" he said and threw his meaty palms skyward as if calling for the Lord.

My aunt corralled the imam beside her, and I set down the barrow and sidled up to my cousin.

In front of our congregation, the intruder continued,

"We questioned day and night, night and day, why you would leave us, Maryam, our Maryam, our Maryam of the Milk! We searched through Y_____ from the tip of the minaret to the cellar of the coffeehouse.

"We found the shepherd's son with a page from your Holy Book, and we beat him and set our dogs at his feet. The shepherd and his sons and their wives took a caravan out of Y_____, and that is when we too began our journey. All of us, all of the Family has come," he exclaimed, gesturing to the throng that trailed him.

"Everywhere we went, we asked, 'have you seen a woman and a young fellow traveling alone? Have you seen a woman who heals and her amber-hued son? A son marked for divinity!' We reconstructed your path, crossing rivers and towns as easily as we once climbed the hillocks of our former homes at the base of the acacia—do you remember it?"

My aunt whispered that she did.

"We came upon your son's doll at an outpost and bartered our jerky for it." He pushed a lanky girl forward. A plum-colored headscarf framed her overcast face. Heavy earrings in the shape of wagon wheels spun as she stepped forward.

This was Ms. A_____. She was resplendent. Glorious. I will not forget how she looked that day. How she appeared. How her appearance into our compound ignited something inside me. It was a feeling I had only felt twice before: when I mounted that steed in the canteen and when the Fanatic had implored me to wrest control of the mosque.

Ms. A_____, it seemed, even in our sunlight existed in shade and shadow. Her eyes were dun-colored. Lips larval. Steel-wool brows. Sorrowful. Sculpted like so few creatures of this world: without a care for virtue! She was like how I imagined the steed Buraq, a beautiful-faced creature!

I shuffled around my cousin to better spy this stately horse of a young lady—the one who shared his mother's breast, who would become the mother of my child. Yes, she would be Faisal's wife—but in name not in deed!

If he was taken with her, Faisal's face remained uncolored, although I did not think to look at him.

Ms. A_____'s hands were unclothed and sinewy, not unfamiliar with toil. Not unlike my own I marveled. She presented the corncob doll to Faisal. He tugged on its tattered arms. Where the corn kernel heart had been, the empty head of a pin shot out.

"But when we heard of a boy who had made water for his people, we knew that it was the beloved son of our beloved Maryam," the man, Ms. A_____'s father, continued. "For who else could perform such a feat? We came here, and we have found you!"

From his shirt pocket, he unfolded a page, as brittle as a vein on a leaf, on which a curved blade separated Ibrahim's and Ismail's distraught forms. "We have returned to you the page of your Holy Book so that you can make it whole and so the Family can again be whole."

As the crowd of Kansans pressed in to glimpse these pilgrims, this Family, Auntie Maryam accepted the rent page from the heavy-set man. Rain came by way of her face.

She thanked him, and then sighed, "I have not thought about those days for some time."

We stood there rapt. Dresses and tunics fluttered in the wind. Crows did not crow, but the goats did their soft bleating.

Ms. A_____'s father asked, "But all this while, while we searched for you, we wondered why, why Maryam of the Milk, why would you leave us? Why did you forsake us and prefer others over us?"

The Family advanced on my aunt, distancing themselves from the Partisan crowd. You could read the betrayal they felt as if it was written on their faces in a script that even an urchined cripple could decipher.

Faisal stepped beside the imam who was surrounded by

these hill people, this Family. They wore their hunger. Even Ms. A_____'s plump father. It carved their chests and their faces and tore at their garments. Even Ms. A_____'s. If the squirrel-faced drover fielded an army, this Family could have been his minions.

I must admit that even as the Family closed in on us, I was overcome with a base appetite in the presence of Ms. A_____. I crossed my iron-beset legs to forestall my awakened sparrow, and the leg braces scraped out a loud and plaintive song like rusted and faulty gears!

It was such a screech that for a moment it diverted the ravenous attention of the rabble away from my aunt and cousin and onto me. And so, the eyes of the crowd were upon my meek and humble and aroused frame. Oh Lord-seated-in-Heaven, I thought, deliver me from their gaze.

My cousin, that boy Faisal, then did something that I, even as I lay here deteriorating in this tower, must admit was remarkable. He knelt at my feet as if I were a divine animal or dignitary in need of a washing. He unbuckled my irons and sequestered my braces. My legs were as barren as the day I was born. And did they ever itch! My toes failed to align, but I recognized them.

"We have come because of him," proclaimed my cousin, which was a truth though seldom acknowledged. "Walk!" commanded Faisal's face, which gleamed as if lit from within.

My own face must have exhibited the dull wonder of curiosity, unsure what theater my cousin was enacting.

"Walk!" he bleated.

I stood there, as our Countrymen exhaled around me and took up my cousin's command. "Walk!" they exclaimed. Then more of them took up the call: "Walk! Walk! Walk boy! Walk! Walk Scrub! Scrub Walk!"

"Walk in the name of the Lord who created you!" bellowed my cousin.

Before I could protest, he shoved me, and I found myself falling—timber!—face-first to the flat Kansan ground. As Country rushed to greet me, my right foot braced my fall. And then, my left.

And before I knew it, my pigeon feet spoke some new winged language! I, who had only ever known how to scrape and shuffle and lurch and wobble—I was running! I was running and a prideful sensation surged through me—the feeling the Prophet must have had when he retook B_____ from the disbelievers!

As I dashed toward the well, I glanced up to see the straw-capped drover seated before me on the ledge. He was distracted by I-know-not-what, staring into the water, and I barreled into him. The man dropped into the drink.

The Brothers first surrendered to applause. Then, the revelry rippled outward. My aunt and the imam, of course, the hungry Family, Ms. A_____ and her father, the miners and finally all the Kansans clapped and trilled in reverence to their new leader: that boy Faisal, the Magician.

Forgotten was the drover who struggled to stay afloat! Disregarded were the plump Family man's inquires! Forgiven was the injustice perpetrated by my aunt on the so-called Family! Neglected was the debility of my appendages! Ignored was the actuality that despite my cousin's showmanship, it was I—not he—who was the one who ran! I was the one who's lame appendages found a new winged tongue!

The Brothers hoisted Faisal above their heads, and they followed the imam as he led the congregation around the well and chanted, "He can heal the sick! He can divine the water!" "He is a doer of right!"

The Family man and his captivating daughter followed them and kissed the black stone as they passed. Would that I was a discolored rock to impugn the lips of my beloved!

As Partisans bumped past me and made their celebratory rounds, circumambulating the well, from the ledge I glowered into the water. The prideful feeling had disappeared. My legs ached from the excursion. And I saw that my leg braces were being passed like a relic from acolyte to acolyte.

The drover, who had braced my flight, struggled in the well. But the trilling of celebrants drowned his howling obscenities. His hat floated beside him like a burst flower.

I dangled my fresh limbs over the edge as the revelers reveled, my sparrow shushed. I fixated on the drover who gasped and bobbed, as unaware that I had been the one to propel him into the well as he was to my spying presence.

A smile bloomed across my face.

I slipped away from the twirling crowd and dragged myself to the minaret on a suckling calf's legs. Liberated from the tyranny of my irons, I no longer sparked the stone as I ascended—ninety-nine, 100, 101—the stairs of my tower.

There, my cagey mind profaned Ms. A_____.

THE NAMES OF THE LORD

Faisal performed one other curative feat before proclaiming that he must, "turn full-time to the proselytizing and not the healing arts."

The drover had shattered a wrist on his plummet into the well. But instead of sinking, as some may have hoped, that foul man treaded water with one arm while the shrieking festivities ensued above him. (From years of beast-lashing, he developed a strong stroke!)

Someone finally heeded his wailing, and the Brothers fished the man out. The bucket of the drover's cap filled with the holy water, and it sunk. (I like to think that among the keepsakes of our civilization, the hat will find its way behind a glass case.)

With a swift hatchet, Faisal did release the man from his affliction, disabling the no longer straw-capped drover's droving. His final healing act concluded, with a detachment of Brothers and his mother's blessings, my cousin ventured to our farthest counties to provoke and inspire.

You will not be surprised to learn that because of Faisal latest marvel, our mosque found yet another form, another incarnation for the devout to glorify the Lord and my cousin. By the time we faced the Missourians at the Ditch, the field behind the mosque had transformed thrice: from ravaged village into barren goat-land, and finally into a boisterous borough as the

Family settled in, mingling their brood with ours.

With the village sprawling at a pace that would give even the most regally bearded cartographer horrors, the bald man that ruled me no longer seeded the field with meat in the mornings. There was hardly space for the flesh to fall and the birds to feed.

Unlike my tame and domesticated self, word of the Plains Prophet traveled, grew feral in that open country, and inspired migrants to undertake the fraught journey to our State. I believe a great number perished in the rust-colored gorges south of Medicine Lodge along the border with the Oklahomans, who are in general an honest lot, though not at all God-fearing.

As in the past, I was compelled to sprinkle rose water on the new arrivals and mask their astringent smell. On mornings after sighting the half moon, I would descend from my minaret on no-longer-constrained limbs into the mosque's canteen to boil the flowers. I grew to loathe them like the baker must his incessant loaves. I can still taste the bitterness of the petals on my hands. Was there anything I regretted more than the smell of harvested roses? Would that there wasn't!

With material cast off from the well's construction, these newly sweet-scented emigrants built their shacks, a tin-roofed bazaar, and a coffeehouse, in which poets recited the doggerel of our days while we sipped on chicory and kindled tobacco.

'Go West!' sang Maryam's heart.
She fled with her Divine son.
Oh Faisal, the Lord has given you the magic
that your mother had.
Heal us—Oh Faisal—Heal us!
With your touch as you did the cripple.

To this day—*the cripple*—the sole acknowledgement in the verse of our land of my role as Chief Groundskeeper and Holy Custodian! Forgive them Lord, for are you not also the Great Forgiver?

The plump Family man secured his daughter, Ms. A_____, as the coffeehouse's proprietress, which precipitated my frequent visits. "Smoke and smolder," I would address my collection of horns and detritus as I quit my tower for the coffeehouse. And it was good: I spent less time in my cloister, which my cousin occupied as he needed to commune with the Lord, or so he said. As if he were a cave dweller in a venerable and timeworn tale!

While I still retained authority as Chief Custodian, the Brothers and their unflagging assistance with all manner of mosque maintenance unmade many of my ministrations. And their ranks swelled with the lengths of their beards! Instructed by the imam and armed with switches—our willow grew bare from over-harvesting, let it not go unsaid—they patrolled the compound. The intended effect was to introduce a measure of order into the sprawling shantytown. But I felt no such security.

These Brothers exhumed the crumbling bollards that demarcated our land and replaced them with forged gates. So, we were now fortified. But did I feel any safer? No, I did not. The menace from without replaced by one from within!

The windows were still pockmarked, but the inside of the mosque, like the outside of the minaret, received fresh white-wash, which finally and forever obscured the Fanatic's blood that had branded my tower.

But I did retain one of my tasks: goat husbandry and, of course, slaughter. The avocation anointed me with additional appellations: the Cripple Butcher, the Mosque Butcher of Kansas, the Cripple Mosque Butcher of Kansas or simply—the Butcher.

This task also, it should not go unsaid, cultivated an imbalance into my body, feeding the meat and sinew of my Raqib or Atid side (who can be sure) in disproportion to the other. One malformity traded for another!

The result was for me dispiriting: I lacked one of the noble qualities detailed in the Holy Book itself! For does not the Lord ask: *"Who created you, then made you complete, then made you symmetrical?"*

And here was I: incomplete and lacking symmetry!

As the imam did with the Brothers, Auntie Maryam ministered to the women. She offered up matronly advice and circulated through the shanties in the drover's cattle cart as he no longer tended it. She taught our women the modesty of her dress, and the Clothed Women, as my aunt's minions called themselves, aped her movements like a clutch does its feathered mother. My aunt's former caretakers, the women from Y_____, assimilated into the Clothed Women and led battalions of their own. They trilled from the bed of the cart as my aunt rode to the ramshackle habitations of a new arrival.

But this was meant to be a tale of my inspiring cousin! How easily I am diverted! For is not the Lord also the One Who Delays Until the Time is Right?

Though I had not been inspired by his sayings, a collection of which no doubt sits unread on the shelf of your own home, one pale morning my cousin divulged to me a story of the Lord, our Lord, which did in me breed no small amount of reflection. The story is as follows: Having scrubbed myself of rosewater, one morning I was on my way to the coffeehouse when I encountered Faisal and the Brothers hitching up a pony trap. I was not called over to assist, but I lingered, drawn by the scent of tobacco, which issued from one of these Sunday soldiers. Upon my approach, a Brother handed me his pouch and a lucifer, though I remained unsure of the reason for his generosity.

I partook, and my cousin sidled up and sipped from my smoke. The chirrs did their thing. A haze in the air stung my eyes, but I recall the day as a pleasant one.

My hands were stained red from a recent sacrifice, and I suppose it made Faisal recall my fresh appellations, which it should be said numbered in the dozens by this time, though I had long ceased counting. My cousin then recounted to me a story about our Lord's many names: "The Almighty," he muttered, "has given Himself ninety-nine names by which we know Him. By which we can call Him."

It was not lost on me that my cousin was in some respects anointing me with the Lord's attributes. And if he was the Plain's Prophet, then what he was saying could not be considered a shirk! Certainly, my names were multitude. So many did I have that our people seemingly could not fathom them— much like the Lord's names!

"There was a hundredth name," Faisal continued, his face rising and falling with the rhythm of his words, beaming or glimmering some might say, "but this Holy Name escaped from the domain of men when a great tower fell. To know that name, to inhabit it, would be to experience the Garden of Immortality."

As we stood there smoking, I reflected on this lesson: To have a name, but also to have no one know it—so like the Lord was I!

I spit out a string of tobacco and chewed on this name, this tower, the congruencies between my circumstances and that of the Lord's.

I asked my cousin, "What was this tower? What was this name?" But he shook his head as if it was an impertinent question and then replied with a firm "hup hup," directed, I would have to guess, at the ponies or the Brothers. He took another sip of my smoke before his party mounted and tore from the mosque, out the new gates, and into the rolling cuestas of our State.

Would that I had removed a pin from the trap's axel, and the ponies tumbled into a ravine! The Lord be praised.

I stubbed out the smoke in a mound of manure, and my mind festered.

What was this Lord's hoarding tower? Was it like my own minaret: reeking and fetid and decorated? Did a reverent custodian inhabit this Lord's name-hoarding tower? Or was it like the steeple of a de-personed church?

Having failed once at giving a name, I still need to know: What was this reverent name?

That morning after the consultation with my cousin, I continued to the coffeehouse where I passed the no-longer drover. He squatted beside the well that had maimed him. His severed wrist had clotted into a hoof-like knot. A court of black flies attended to it. This: my cousin's magic.

The man's remaining hand was outstretched in the fashion of a beggar, and he seemed unperturbed by my form. If he suspected my role in his disfigurement, he didn't divulge it in an appropriate, brutish manner. A congealed bowl of meat porridge donated by a congregant rested beside him. Several worshippers passed the man as they stroked the obsidian rock wedged into the well by my cousin. They kissed their fingers and attested to the Lord's greatness. I did the same, and then quit for the coffeehouse.

There, I cut through curtains of sweet smoke and found a seat nearest my love, Ms. A_____, who labored in the galley. The few patrons sipped from their water pipes in unhurried rumination, as if we weren't at war.

Ms. A_____ procured for me a pipe and a tin cup of chicory coffee. I nodded at her in thanks, and although wordlessly she shuffled away, I could tell that my cup was filled higher than the other groveling patrons. And she had crumbled sugar into it already! And she had even stirred it!

But I could not linger on my affections. No, the Lord's name-hoarding tower still occupied my cagey mind! And What was His unheard, unseen, unwitnessed name? What was it?

Though I was disabled, I am still man enough to admit that my plots did not work out as I had planned. However, I am convinced that I am closer to the Lord's missing name than is my cousin seated now in Heaven.

THE BROWN MEN

When the man Brown arrived with his sons, I had ventured to the dry riverbed that corralled our compound. (There was no Lote tree for those still striving for knowledge, but perhaps there was a Zaqqum and its fiery harvest?) Although it lengthened the journey, I had kept to the forest's edge and avoided the village that sprawled like a supplicant behind the mosque. The whole place to me was no better than kindling. Gnats bobbed behind me, while a gentle air impelled me onwards.

I didn't know where the graves of my parents were or even if they had graves, but when I had last trundled through the area, I uncovered a patch of barren, russet earth and suddenly fought nausea. I thought that maybe my parents or perhaps a parent had been buried there, and so I performed a return pilgrimage.

Although I was healed, my appendages, long inured to the support of the iron braces, cramped from the excursion. For this you are thanked, Faisal.

The ground was tough, unyielding, as if paved with hooves. From the riverbed, I salvaged stones and hid them in the pockets of my tattered tunic where they replaced the copper pellets I had once hoarded. I scratched away until I exhumed a skull-sized mound. From a satchel, I unwrapped the liver of a goat and buried it. Then, I raised a hand to my pursed lips and kissed my fingers. Into the wind, I spoke the prayer: *To Him we belong and to Him we shall return.* For He is the Ever Surviving One. It was a good ceremony, but rain did not come by way of my face.

The funeral completed, I made my way back to my minaret where I found our clucking citizenry swarming a carriage in the mosque's front lot like hens to seed. I had seen carriages but never one as elegant—as if sculpted from polished stone!

A stout Brother guarded the men's entrance and harangued supposed infiltrators as if he was a qualified judge. "Brown and sons to greet us," he offered, and a smile broke his face. I too spied on the arrivals as they dismounted the carriage.

Why the man was called Brown I did not know. He did not retain a hue but what had seared his skin. He and his brood were renowned for their cunning and exploits against unbelievers, peculiar institutions. Honored is what we were by their presence though we did not act like it. No, we acted like tenderfoots was what we acted like.

Brown and sons brushed by me as they entered the mosque. They wore wool suits with buttons of gold or brass, which was befitting—rumors of their wealth had penetrated our cloister. But the wool was unfitting for the swelter, which wilted us that day.

The Browns were lean, sinewy, and a broadsword dangled from the elder's belt. They had straightness to them, a symmetry! These were men to which we could aspire! Small-eyed, yes, but steely, the color of rifle barrels. The elder Brown, a frail man of nearly a century, had a beard that split due to its length! A dignified cloak of hair meant to disguise him, but by which we all knew of him. As if a beard could be used for dissemblance!

I stroked the down of my own face and nearly crowed as the Browns removed their boots, revealing a half-dozen hairless feet! They were quickly cleansed by a team of bucket-and-sandalwood-soap-wielding Brothers with a precision that rivaled my own, save they were faster, their hands nimbler, and they worked in unison. It was a sight.

The visitors slipped into the mosque, where the imam

greeted them in the prayer room, wishing them peace. Partisans charged behind in the interminable shuffling of devotees. The imam's own beard faded to the verdigris of the mosque's dome when confronted by the glory that was the elder Brown's! At this I did crow, though Bahira was not appreciative of my laughter, which he made known by glowering at me.

My aunt instructed me to fetch my cousin and coffee for the guests. I found that fellow asleep, slumped over Bahira's desk, quill in hand. I slapped his knit kufi, and as he startled awake, I presented the cap back to him, my palms exposed.

Weaving through the crowd—how easy it was for me to avoid the tricksters with my quick feet!—I sought the canteen. Clothed Women brewed chicory. I carried the drink on a pewter platter and presented it to the Browns with a deep bow.

In a hoarse voice that sounded like dried corn husks rubbed together, the elder man mangled out speech. When he coughed, which was often, the sons alternated with translation: They warned of attack and occupation. Of annexation and annihilation. Of towns burned and razed. Of overrun rivers and slaughtered children, women too.

We had heard their tales before, I thought. By men more fearsome, though less distinguished.

A phalanx of Brothers crowded around my cousin, who clapped the elder Brown's shoulders and assured the men that we were willing to take up arms against the Missourians. But, he warned them, we were lacking in the arms that we were willing to uptake. With Maryam by his side, even Bahira seemed to acquiesce to my cousin's offer and request, but the screeching, clucking, and buzzing of our fearful disciples nearly drowned it out! As I have said, we acted like tenderfoots was what we acted like.

I recalled the Jay-hawker Fanatics who had courted us, to whom I had offered my fealty, who had advised me to take over the mosque. *To Him we shall return*, I thought.

Faisal led the men into the imam's office. With the crowd, I dispersed, and retired to the coffeehouse. My pockets still laden with riverbed stones.

Before the bilal sang the call for the evening prayer, rumor had spread that a plan to combat the Missourians had been devised, and we rushed back into the mosque. The Browns had joined Faisal, who had changed into vestments, at the foot of the minbar. Then we prayed—though I was certain that I was not the only congregant who had his thoughts on matters other than the Lord!

After prayer, Faisal regaled us with a story that in one form or another we had all heard....

THE MISSOURIANS

When Missourians crept into his house and marched up the stairs to his bedroom, they found him asleep, wrapped in the royal blue of our flag. The Prophet secured a curved blade from a trembling Bushwhacker. He clutched the man's long locks and exposed the soft meat of the would-be murderer's throat. He made urchins of the terrorist's children and a widow of his wife.

SUNFLOWER STATE ZINDABAD

As if struck by a true magician's wand, our listless citizens leapt with a fanatical fury. Shouts of "God is great!" and "Sunflower State zindabad!" broke out in a freshet after Faisal's screed. The Lord be praised!

With their experience fighting infidels, Brown's sons—the buttons of their suits sparkling—instructed my cousin's goons on how to fortify the mosque compound. The Brothers unrolled cutting wire atop the gates and planted land torpedoes in the forest beside the minaret—a trick the sons had gleaned from the terrorists themselves, which produced for us several martyrs in the process. For this was the sorrowful ciphering of internecine warfare.

The Browns armed the Brothers and the Clothed Women with the Springfields they had smuggled in the bed of their carriage. The miners contributed kegs of powder, and for my part, I crammed round stones into a buttressed cattle cart. Would that stones were a subject for poetry.

The visitors stayed with us in a shack built behind the coffeehouse—the shack that would become my cousin's and his wife's home for nearly an evening. And while his sons and the Brothers toiled, Brown the elder regarded the poets in the coffeehouse.

I often gleaned a seat nearest him and scrubbed country

from his weathered feet as he attempted to regale us with tales of hardship and privation, also of crusade. The mushrooms of his throat obscured the narrative, but I sat in rapt attention when he would divulge his travels: He spoke to us of beautiful, bountiful Colorado, where the mountains floated like tufts of sheared wool! Spring-waters and floods! A place where anyone could find a crag in which to commune with the All-Knowing Lord! And Colorado was just across our State—in the opposite compass from the Missourians! The Lord with all His ninety-nine names did provide!

The mosque fortified by these men, there was one task that remained before our Partisans journeyed east to confront the would-be occupiers: Auntie Maryam directed the Clothed Women in The Task of Sewing. She commanded her minions to embrace the needle-and-thread and embroider their husbands' or sons' or daughters' clothing with verses from the Holy Book. It was a protection ruse, and it gave us hope.

One night, dizzied by the dual intoxicants of tobacco and verse, I quit the coffeehouse and lifted a pair of pajamas that hung on a washerwoman's line. Stitched along a seam was the inscrutable phrase: *"They ask thee of new moons, say: They are fixed seasons for mankind and for the pilgrimage."*

Perhaps, it was then that I should have made my escape, my season for pilgrimage. Colorado—filled with the Lord's Bounty—I shall never find you!

On a visit to my chambers atop the minaret, my cousin disclosed to me the march to the Kawsmouth: The onslaught would commence from the muddied and barricaded banks of the Missouri River!

The day came for the procession to advance, and I adorned a fine and able steer in the flag of our Country and slapped its hide as we proceeded into the yard in front of the mosque. For reasons undivulged to my person, the Brothers had costumed one of their own in a stiff suit of woven straw. Fearsome he was not, but that was the intended effect—as I have said Missourians are known cowards. The costumed Brother marched behind the steer as he could. His stiff-legged adversity provoked memories of my own.

We joined the imam and onlookers as my cousin, deco-rated in a heavy suit that aped the Browns', decamped the mosque to join the combatants. The imam stuck two fingers into his mouth and let forth a sharp whistle. A team of Brothers then emerged from behind the mosque with a glorious, white-washed steed. It was a forgery, but it was a white horse just as the imam had once sermoned that the Redeemer would ride!

A resolute Brother gave my cousin a boost, and he mounted the animal with far less adversity than I had with my horse. Though come to think of it, that whitewashed nag courted the same afflictions, a rent ear and a clouded eye, as mine had! They had given him my own horse!

The paint streaked Faisal's suit, but he uttered thankful praises. The manufactured Redeemer, the Commander of the Faithful, it seemed, had arrived, relying on his own judgment and the unseen hand of Providence. Brothers trilled and drowned out the chirrs. The Lord be praised.

"He is of the stuff of which martyrs are made," the elder Brown choked out, and his grin blossomed into an ugly thing on his face. (We would learn later that Brown was hanged after taking the fight eastward, and when I think of him, the image of his contorted, smiling face, masked with that magnificent beard, is what I see.)

After he mounted the horse, Faisal let out a cry, "If the Lord be for us, who can be against?" Talut, who it should not be forgotten also tested his faithful by a river, would have been proud.

The mosque compound emptied of souls who were not me, including Brown and his sons, who anointed the battalion as the Kansas Provisional Army. Laden cattle carts and the Clothed Women serried behind them. The Black Goat, as the Brothers had taken to calling the former drover, shuffled alongside. He struggled against the weight of a water pot, which was lashed to his back by a swath of burlap. He bleated out "water, water" in a plaintive way.

Even the pulpy Family man joined the procession. But thankfully, his daughter, Ms. A_____, remained to tend to the coffeehouse and to spur my affections!

The elderly, the tenderfoots, the left women, and my humble self showered the procession with the stunted gold of sunflower petals. Cries of "Sunflower State zindabad!" churned through the air. A stalky Brother sang a mournful nasheed, while another knocked on a goatskin drum. The slanting sun and a phalanx of horned beasts bid the battalion farewell.

My aunt clanged shut the gates of the mosque as she exited. Through the bars, she gestured for me to approach. Impregnable we were not.

There was no tenderness to her fading face. No suspicion that she might not return, that this skirmish or battle or whatever would transpire would culminate in casualties irrespective of the outcome. I have found it was such with Fanatics.

Auntie Maryam grasped my hands with her blotchy ones. "Now, you are the one who is in charge," she said.

I wish I could say that pride bloomed in my meager form. But it did not.

Instead, nausea overcame me. Perhaps the dyspepsia that struck obscured more meaningful sentiments.

I retreated into the crowd of undesirables, watching the combatants shuffle away, uncertain of their return but certain that theirs was the correct path, the true path.

Then I scurried—scurried!—into my tower and spied the so-called Provisionals from an arrowslit until they were nothing but a trail of fire ants on their way to a fleshy harvest.

I was, at least until my cousin and the imam returned—
if they would return—in charge of the mosque! The desired
outcome took longer to achieve than I had hoped, and my
ascension was less sanguinary than I had envisioned. But nevertheless, it was public, unquestionable and unimpeachable.

Unsure of what else to do, I retired to my chambers to
interrogate the Holy Book.

How I wish I could have called upon our Fanatics to aid me!

In the absence of that cousin boy, my attempts to minister
to the depopulated mosque were met not with the sustained
applause and reverence I expected, but by the rasping and
wheezing of the decrepit! The few who could be bothered
to join me in the prayer hall could have at best been termed
remnants. While my counsel was sought, settling disputes
between the elderly required far more contemplation than I
wished to undertake!

And so, days after our regiment decamped I quit the
mosque and instead patrolled the many forking paths of our
desolate compound with a switch of my own devising. I found
the barren earth of my parents' or perhaps parent's gravesite
and near it cultivated certain analgesic seasonings procured for
me by a passing spiritualist. I termed it my Garden of Immortality. I also bedded down the animals in my keep and explored
the habitations of my guardians, retrieving a rifle and satchel of
copper pellets from the imam's chambers, with which I used to
snipe at cottontails that made for a scrumptious harvest.

There was one other thing: While many shopkeepers had
shuttered their stalls to join the frontline, the coffeehouse
remained open. And there, under the crossbeams of its low
roof, I exhaled braids of smoke and spied on Ms. A_____ in
my cousin's absence.

My beloved could hardly heft the glass water pipes and

samovars! Instead, she dragged them across the grit floor, carving a map of her labor into the disagreeable grounds, which I happily followed like an earnest cartographer! I almost never met her eyes with my own, but in my memory they were pale green, the color of wilted grass. And I did my part, returning the used pipes, cups, and cutlery to the scullery. Once, I believe, I even elicited a smile from Ms. A____, and it should come as no surprise when I tell you I pleasured myself to that memory on many an occasion.

THE HUNDREDTH STEP

Assisted by the analgesic seasonings I had husbanded near my parents' or perhaps parent's graves, I had taken to an uncolored sleep while the warriors were away warring. It was glorious, and the kind of slumber I associated with men who knew their side triumphant!

But one morning after the Provisionals had left, I startled awake to Missourian war cries! Or so I thought. That a trickle of piss irrigated my trousers will also come to you as no surprise, but it did make the minaret reek.

I cradled the imam's pellet rifle and emerged from my tower into the clamor. After a fortnight or perhaps two fortnights, they all had returned from the Battle of the Ditch unscathed—save for a score of martyrs whose unrecorded names rust on the banks of the Kaw. These triumphants had brought the trilling, which would continue for weeks, well into the Festival of Sacrifice. I had mistaken their celebrations for the hooting of Bushwhackers. It was a common mistake, one that must have bedeviled even the most steadfast Partisan.

I spied my cousin on his no-longer-white horse. But gleaming was what he was. He laughed and glad-handed Brothers as if slaughter was not a thing that any man should shy away from or fear. Yes, I did envy him at that moment. Yes, I did raise the rifle and aim it in the neighborhood of his head. And yes, the weapon did fire, but it was a weak rebellion as the pellet sailed so far from his person that it only inspired others to fire their rifles into the vault in celebration! So, in my own way I did contribute to the festivities—as I should have.

"Where were the Brown men?" I asked a ragged-looking Brother, who seemed to have taken a blade somewhere tender and was wrapped quite heavily.

They had quit our territory to take the fight east, he revealed, and *"to Him we shall return,"* I thought. Thankfully, I found the steer unharmed and corralled our flag for future conflagrations.

As the battalion streamed in, they kissed the mosque's gates, and it occurred to me that my tenure as mosque chieftain had expired with nary a mortar fired nor a land torpedo detonated, except those by inadvertent ungulates. How weak had been my tenure? I had even lost kids to a predatory wolf until it too was consumed by a land torpedo!

To celebrate our victory, speeches commenced, proclamations were declared, and the Governor of our State publicly reverted to Mahomatism. And yes, much feasting occurred, which required the roasting of the remainder of my herd. And so, I retreated to my familiar second home, the shed, with a whetted blade.

My non-goat-slaughter time I spent, where else, in the coffeehouse, where I indulged on pipe and honeyed tea until Ms. A_____ parted the twin worms of her lips and bleated our boastful ballads. In the absence of the others and to my delight, Ms. A_____ had mastered the soft-warbling skills of the poets. And it was from her that I discovered what transpired at the Kawsmouth from the flowing tongue of my love as she sang The Song of the Battle of the Ditch:

When Faisal reached the west bank, he tied a
Green sash around his head

And smeared his cheeks with our soil.

Oh Faisal, how did you know to inspire us?
He sent the miners upstream and
The straw Brother into the fore
And when the Missourians boarded their vessels
To cross the innocent river and occupy Our Land
They saw the fearsome strawman and it filled
Their hearts with terror.

For Missourians are known Cowards!

Faisal's tongue gave out its call!
Oh Faisal, how did you know to call?

The miners blew the bank!
They staunched the mighty waters!

As they dropped into the riverbed,
the Missourians scrambled this-way-and-that!

For Missourians are known Cowards!

And then did a cannonade of stones rain down
And crushed them so they floundered like fish.

Oh Faisal, have the Browns ever seen a fighter such as you?

Oh Faisal, how true was your aim, which men did you brain?

The Missourians fought with their rifles from deep in the ditch.
A spark lit the strawman!
He ascended to the Heavens ablaze.

And we thank you martyrs of the Ditch
And we will join you in the Garden
When the Lord asks.

Oh Faisal, prepare us for that day!

Then did the Missourians scale the west bank.
Then did Faisal give out another cry.
And then did the miners blow the dammed river
So once again it flowed across that vile and cave-ridden state.
Sweep the Missourians into the Mississippi, oh Lord!

Oh Faisal, when you returned to us, a hero in your own Land,
Did you know how we loved you?

Each time Ms. A_____ versified her admiration for my cousin, a pain tore me like a tufted hawk at my liver. I assuaged my anguish by adulterating the tobacco with my analgesic seasoning. In a misremembered episode occasioned by my indulgence, I may have vigorously protested her crooning. I do not recall the incident, but that gluttonous Family man barred me from the coffeehouse for one mournful week.

But I was undeterred! An inspired and fanatical man will find a way to inebriate himself on the words of his beloved! Days into my banishment, I lifted a Clothed Woman's laundered cloak and headscarf from the washer line. As they do, I wrapped and wrapped the diaphanous fabric around my head until only the murky moons of my eyes shone through. So disguised, I cheated back into the coffeehouse—the first but not the last time I camouflaged myself in this manner. As I have mentioned, I was resolute, steadfast, and many other benedictions.

But if hearing my love profess her love for another was a never-ending agony, witnessing her betrothal and then marriage to my triumphant cousin-now-planted-in-Heaven was like a hooded torture that I was certain the Lord, in His benevolence, leaves unnamed. For He is the Benevolent One.

They conducted the betrothal after a Prophet's Day prayer. At the front of the prayer hall, the regal pair, my cousin and my beloved Ms. A_____, were dressed in fine raiment and abided one another as if they had not been acquainted, glancing coyly at each other and then away. At each other and then away.

Rain came by way of tributes. The imam gave his blessings, before Auntie Maryam and the Family man vociferated theirs with a passion typically reserved for a ta'ziya as if this match was ordained decades ago in a virulent town. They took turns recounting tales from Y_____ and proceeded to bore us with the particulars of their first encounter as if we hadn't heard the stories before!

A season passed, frost to seedtime, before the loathed match was loathly conjoined. For the nuptials, I was delegated a responsibility to which I was accustomed—our herd having been replenished by generous shepherds from across the State. Would that I had had a less murderous vocation to court. The Lord be praised.

My cousin was to deliver a sermon the day before the ceremony. I intended to confront him in front of the assembled masses with a litany of his duplicitousness, which I had catalogued and retained in my steely mind, to reveal his ineffectuality and disabuse the gathered of his noble conception—and by doing so, terminate the ceremony!

Was I not the one who tended to the mosque? Was I not the one who found the snake? Was I not the one whose game found the well? Was I not the one with nearly as many names as the Lord? Was I not The One?

I awoke early, before the miners blustered, and corralled

the goats. Beasts, as anyone knows, share a bond with their masters, and they too were anxious—the gravity of the day weighing heaviest on those who have no agency with which to confront it. So, it was for their sake that I maintained a deliberate and placid manner while exsanguinating the scores that were needed for the wedding party, breaking only for smokes, sips of well-water, and oatcakes.

As midday loomed, I relinquished my duties and knives to the Brothers and shambled into the coffeehouse to plot the confrontation. My warbling muse was unpresent—a team of Clothed Women no doubt preparing her for the nuptials. (What tinctures they must use!) and the ensuing celebratory feast. Her lack of presence I found a preoccupation as distracting as her feeble yet enchanting presence!

I compensated by medicating myself with far more of my Garden of Immortality than I had intended. The indulgence conspired with my goat-weariness to obscure my resolute mind and to transform my regal and unencumbered appendages into syrupy ones.

But I did manage to shuffle into the prayer hall as my cousin commenced storifying!

In what would be his final sermon, Faisal addressed the issue of the welts on his back. The defect, he claimed, was as Bahira suspected—a mark of divinity. A besmirchment, he suggested, he shared with those Bearded Enchanters of our Histories. He spoke of a dream in which, he averred, a pair of wings sprouted from the discoloration. On these wings he flew, he asserted, to our capital, where he met the Archangel who extended to him a silver platter of palm dates stuffed with almonds and a cannikin of milk, which was warm. The angel's milk tasted no saltier than our own, he divulged, inciting our devotees and eliciting boisterous approvals. From the capital's cathedral, he and the Archangel ascended to the cloudless Heavens, he insisted.

The Black Goat perceived a distress in my cousin as he spoke of ascending to Heaven, and the inconsiderate man thrust out a tin of water with his able hand. Faisal sipped as consciousness lost its firm grip on me, and I thumped to a prayer rug as I was capable of doing.

I quickly righted myself and shrieked, "You confound truth with falsehood!" And then was apprehended by a persevering pair of branch-wielding goons in matching skull caps, who dragged me out of the mosque!

Would that the Lord had devised less cunning intoxicants with which to ensnare us.

But if it were not for the Lord's cunning intoxicants, would I have come to the vital conclusion? Would I have executed the desired and long-awaited plot?

Exhale as you say it: *In the name of the Almighty, Gracious, and most Merciful Lord.*

After my outburst at the sermon, the not-so-benevolent Brothers deposited me on the ledge at the base of the minaret, lashing me, yes, but unseverely. The night chuffed roosting animals, who mimicked my moans and cries, and what I thought were clouds obscured a sliver moon.

Drowsy and nauseous from my overindulgence on Garden of Immortality seasoning, I counted the steps as I ascended my tower: one, two, three… ten, eleven, twelve… twenty-one, twenty-two, twenty-three… thirty-four, thirty-five, thirty-six…

The clouds revealed themselves.

thirty-eight, thirty-nine, forty…

A blimp obscured the moon.

forty-one, forty-two, forty-three… fifty-seven, fifty-eight, fifty-nine…

and then another…

seventy-three, seventy-four, seventy-five…

eighty-eight, eighty-nine, ninety…

How many were they?

ninety-one, ninety-two, ninety-three…

Here for me?

ninety-four, ninety-five, ninety-six…

Here for me?

ninety-seven, ninety-eight, ninety-nine…

At that moment, I stopped.

The final step into my chamber was not the one-hundred-and-first!

I had miscounted on my arrival into the minaret and had taken the miscounting to be correct. As I have said I was not a scholar!

The final step was the hundredth.

Ninety-nine, and I lifted first one emancipated foot and then the other—one-hundred! It was the hundredth step. I was the hundredth step.

Despite or perhaps because of my bleariness, I had arrived at the necessary and portentous conclusion. And the blimps, those fat gorgeous creatures, the blimps had returned to celebrate my ascendance. And to announce it!

And I, F_____, not *Faisal,* was the hundredth name.

F_____—the Lord's name!

F_____—the Redeemer!

For is He not also the Redeemer?

How else to interpret this divine sign? This divine guidance bequeathed to my humble self in the form of man's purest and untainted language—that of numbers! Of the simple act of counting, which any tenderfoot could ascertain.

For the Lord loves a perfect symmetry!

How else to account for the words whispered in my tower? In my room!

How else to explain the indifference to my own names? Scrub? Brush? Tree? Cripple? Butcher?

How else to interpret the ineptitude of our peoples with

respect to their ability to recall or remember my name? Their defect was not with them! They could not see my name, they could not hear it—they could not know it! The Lord safekept this name from them as He must!

As I entered the perch atop the minaret and spied the blimp-clotted sky, I knew what must be done to reclaim the Good Lord's Name. And it would begin with a return to my Garden of Immortality.

That night, I fell asleep to the cacophony of fruit bats. Their commotion battered the small circle of my room.

The next day, the wedding day, I galloped—galloped!—down the winding stone staircase. I looked above me. Where else would you look? The blimps had departed, but I took that as a good sign.

Like a qualified pioneer, I hiked along the edge of the forest, weary of the land torpedoes sown like vengeful seeds by the Brown brothers to safeguard us from the terrorists. When I reached my Garden of Immortality, I removed my tunic to reveal unblemished shoulders. I harvested the clinging seasoning and bundled it into the cloth.

In the mosque, an arrangement, a pact, papers stamped with Kansas Nuptials Department were signed with plumed pen to register the matrimony. The imam conducted what I understood to be an abbreviated ceremony in his office before he, my cousin, the Family man, and my aunt led a dancing-and-trilling line of colorful dancers and trillers into the coffeehouse where awaited the bride.

While the ceremony and celebration transpired, in my tower's entryway I ground the herbs with mortar and pestle until I was bearded in the stuff. Then I cleansed myself with well-water before joining the celebrants—the pockets of my shirt stuffed with sweet-scented seasonings.

Veiled in the golden color of our State's flower, Ms.

A_____ greeted her husband at the coffeehouse's corrugated entryway. She made music with each step, her anklets rattling and tinkling. Their celebratory din evoked the copper pellets I had once hoarded. My love, even on her wedding night to another, incited a smile on my lightly bearded face.

Honeyed milk and mulled tea flowed as the Family man invited the village to celebrate. We indulged on salted beef and simmered goat, fry bread, cornbread, oatcake. Skins of perfumed well-water quenched us. Baskets of cider cakes and berries sweetened our salaams. Oil lamps sputtered out their warmth. Poets warbled, and drums roared, though I was spared from hearing my love call the praises of my cousin, her momentary husband. Even the Black Goat retired the water-pot for the evening and joined the gaieties, drowning in the sweet milk and wolfing down the meats. Smoke from water pipes roiled the coffeehouse, and becapped Brothers brandished reed fans to disperse the stormy air.

But on this promising and incipient evening, I refrained from the dark indulgences!

I cornered that cousin boy and offered my tidings to disabuse the celebrants of their concerns regarding my questionable presence, if they had any. My good fortune found the imam and my aunt engulfed in well-wishers, too preoccupied for me to add sustained attentions.

After much deliberate, some might say, vigorous malingering, I removed my person from the proceedings—the lack of my presence would go unnoticed, of this I was certain. I hunted for the steadfast washer line and once again donned the cloak and headscarf of a Clothed Woman, though there were no protecting words sewn inside.

Returning to the jubilee, I announced my transformed and unrecognizable presence with vocal and sustained trilling. My tongue flapped until my voice matched the Brown man's in vile hoarseness!

In this costume, I hid as the festivities endured and threatened to outlast even the most obstinate of the night's stars. From beneath my cloak, I spied the Brothers taking leave of the celebration or slumping over in their chairs, asleep. Their heads tilted back and exposed the soft meat of their throats.

I encountered a water pipe, moss-green glass that had been adorned in that ancient script—a gift to the remarkable couple. Into the earthenware head I packed the Garden of Immortality and a pinch of tobacco and lit the pipe with an asthenic match.

The feted settled at a banquet table nearest the coffee-house's galley. As a Clothed Woman, I again approached my love and my cousin unmolested and hefted the offering on the table as if it were my own tribute. They would not refuse, and the couple even thanked me for the consideration! After both had sipped and sputtered out smoke, I offered them another sip. They indulged again, and once more before I swept in and removed the pipe, emptying the head into an ash pan.

The Clothed Women and I watched as stumbling Partisans dispersed into their hushed homes or back into the mosque, which without my meager assistance had been converted into a sort of festive barracks so that travelers could slumber there after the festivities.

Finally, my aunt's battalion dispersed when she quit the celebration. As they left, I smuggled myself into a pantry closet from where I could spy on the dwindling party. That pulpy Family man embraced my cousin, his temporary son-in-law, whose well-nourished presence as an infant had birthed this sect. He then clutched his daughter between his meaty arms with such delight that you could nearly forgive him for being captivated with my aunt those many years ago. It was a tender scene full of tears and soft-hearted flattery.

What does a father reveal to his child on a wedding night? I was certain that it was not dissimilar to the prayers exhaled by a cripple butcher before he transformed breath to flesh. *There there now.*

With a pack of Brothers, the Family man then fled into the near dawn, while I remained cloistered. As sunlight cheated through the obscured coffeehouse, Faisal fell asleep atop a table. Precipitated by our conference with the water pipe and surrounded by platters of shredded goat meat, his body resigned itself to sleep, as though sleep is only dream. The fat from the meat congealed around him.

Though wearied herself by the seasoning, Ms. A_____ approached my cousin and attempted to shake her provisional partner awake, trying to coax him into their conjugal bedroll with luscious whisperings. My diminutive love failed in her attempts—how the mighty are unenslaved by the endearments of the meek!—and alone she made her stumbling way to the shack once built for the Browns. Her lurching and scraping movements mimicked my own disablement in the years before my cousin's healing trickery. A smile broke across my face.

A short and narrow alley connected the matrimonial shack to the coffeehouse. But before reaching the bedroom, the seasoning took hold of Ms. A_____, and she tumbled to the grit floor. Such was the potency of my Garden that even children of the wilderness raised in a makeshift village on the outskirts of a diseased town fell prey!

Pressed against sacks of dried chicory, I exhaled the clear steam of the righteous into the storage closet. No animal, not even a Brother, stirred.

I tiptoed—yes—I tiptoed around a sleeping Brother and leapt! over noxious, pipe-water puddles. If I had had a disability, you would not have known it in that moment.

I reached the waist-high table on which my cousin rattled and snored. The sleeves of his embroidered tunic sopped up the meat juices around him. His heavy head crushed his golden turban. He was a sight—like an angel crashed down.

I rolled up the sleeves of my Clothed Women's gown. From the floor, I snatched a towel and wrapped it around my right hand like a pugilist. With my non-wrapped hand, I, for the first but not the last time, parted my cousin's jaws. He did not wake. I snaked my cloth fist into his mouth. So close to me that he inhaled my acrid and sustaining exhalations.

I whispered my name, "F_____, F_____," into his face, as I suffocated his fine and beaked and unbloodied nose with my free hand. I leaned my full weight into him, pressing, it seemed, all the air out. I deflated him with my frailty like a stake into a goat bladder pouch.

Then, I waited while he soured on the table. My pilfered headscarf fluttered to the floor, revealing my nearly hairy countenance.

It took longer than I might have suspected, but eventually his eyes came to. They shivered, and then his chest heaved. Consciousness found him, and he jolted awake.

I met his bewilderment with my immutable stare. In the shallow wells of his ears I confided my name, the Lord's name: "F_____, F_____, F_____."

"For is He not also the Redeemer?" I asked.

Faisal fluttered, and his eyes clouded though I saw the outlines of an unfamiliar sapling pass through them.

Then, my cousin, the so-called Plains Prophet, Commander of the Faithful, tried to chaw my fist! But his mouth, with my hand in it, was stretched far too wide for such an assault. His fingernails sliced into the flesh of my neck, but at that moment, I was the resolute son, the son named after the Lord.

He heaved on the table and lunged his person at me. Bits of meat scattered, and a serving plate crashed. But I countered with my meager weight and with my suspect appendages. And for a moment I had tamed him like an oblivious kid in the slaughter shed!

He continued flailing, and it seemed improbable that I would be left unthrown. Rather, it seemed apparent that my person would be dislodged, Brothers aroused, and a swift and brutal justice administered without even a qadi to articulate in my defense!

We interweaved limbs with a warring intensity, and I called on the steely determination I had mustered to tame that wild steed!

And I succeeded—I succeeded!—in pacifying my cousin's torment with my calloused hands! The Lord be praised!

Faisal then did a thing that I'm not certain I had ever witnessed in my years of slaughter: His dusky eyes peered into my own, but they had quit of fury. Instead, they shone. They shone with something like a calmness. He seemed to resist my advances by not resisting, resigning instead like a spiritless poltroon and allowing his hands to drop in peaceful protest.

He had then two countenances: the outward one still as if in a dream. The one beneath it, rage-filled.

"There there now," I whispered. "There there now."

He made water, staining his wedding tunic and the Clothed Woman's cloak I had donned and adding to the mess on the table. 'Oh, enemy of the Lord,' I thought, 'I will give thee no respite!' (I thought that, but I did not repeat it out loud.) I wanted him to feel my hand clenched around the dirty rag inside the cavity of his throat.

His chest gave a final spasm that jarred the platters! But my thoughts drifted to Prophet Ibrahim as he held his firstborn child down and held his blade aloft.

I scanned the room. If there were iridescent men, I did not see them. But a spout of sunlight did for a moment obscure my eyesight and a fan fell from the grasp of a sleeping Brother onto the puckered ground.

I pulled my shrouded hand from Faisal's mouth and tossed the rag into a puddle. I massaged my forearm and neck, where Faisal had left a sermon in my tender flesh. Sweat and piss stained my misbegotten cloak, and I slumped into my cousin's seat to comport myself.

Faisal's eyes were still wide, though they were dull and indeed lifeless. There were no clouds, no tenements, no flowing trees in them. I shut them with the V of my fingers. I whispered my name, "F_____," one last time and then slipped the imam's prayer beads from around his neck, draping them on my own. I removed the crushed turban from under his head, and I wore it myself. My Lord, I thought, it fits.

My cousin splayed on the table in an obscene, some might say undignified, manner. So, I tended to him: placed his arms at his side, straightened his befouled garments, and shifted him so that he might better face the Holy Cube to which we pray.

Having helped my cousin, I diverted my attentions back to my beloved, bumping through the coffeehouse until I reached her slumped form in the alleyway that led to the shack. Finally, I thought, Ms. A_____ and I were to have our clandestine conference! For does not a brother inherit his departed sibling's wives? Was not a brother's duty to give a child to the childless wife of his brother? Was Faisal not like a brother to me?

I carried her to the bedchambers, where I could see that Clothed Women had adorned the mattress with petals and stalks of unthreshed wheat in a matrimonial fashion. River sand had been strewn about the earthen floor in a fertility ruse that I had attempted successfully with my herd. It seemed like a lark conjured up by the desperate imaginations of the barren, but it sure worked!

Ms. A_____'s heft and girth were substantial, more than I had anticipated, and I wondered if it weren't better to just lay her next to my sleeping cousin so that they could have this night together.

I quickly thought better of it. I don't know why that thought had entered my mind, as it was quite the opposite of what I intended. But who knows how the cagey mind works? As I have said, I was not a shaman or healer of any sort. In this, I did differ from my cousin.

And so, I laid Ms. A_____ on the canopied bedroll with a shepherd's lack of grace. Luckily, she did not at that moment stir, but her unruly and pale curls eluded her head scarf. I tucked them behind her ears and snuck a wet kiss on her fat lips. A trail of spittle connected us, until I broke away my face from hers.

I removed the Clothed Woman's cloak I had been wearing and relieved the twine cinching my trousers. Save for my cousin's crown and the prayer beads, I was as naked as the day my mother bore me!

Then, I turned my attentions to my unconscious consort. In truth, I had a difficulty removing her garments. Women's nuptial clothing, it turned out, was chock-full of latches, buttons, and other contraptions as if to deter the true purpose of the ceremony—and that was obviously the engendering of a new life! It was what separated us from the animals—that we marked our occasions with contracts and festivities.

And so, I simply rent the fabric of her own trousers, if women could be said to wear them, before I proceeded to try and lay with her.

She was unmoving at first, and I had to manipulate both her person and my sparrow to achieve the desired effect!

Despite the consoling prowess of the Garden of Immortality, Ms. A_____ did bleat something incomprehensible to my thrusting self. I corralled her hands and stroked my face with them as I had learned to do in reverse to placate harvest goats.

"There there now," I whispered. "There there now."

I pressed my Jupiter finger against her lips. This motion both seemed to temper Ms. A_____, and yet it also aroused in her a fierce appetite: Either it was a struggle to free herself from my person, or it was the opposite for her one leg wrapped quite nearly around me and slapped across my backside. In its way, it reminded me of my tussle with that steed in the mosque's canteen or even of my warring with my deceased cousin for I feared being thrown yet again!

The skirmish for a moment diminished my ardor, and I thought perhaps I should quit her. But then, I called upon a reserve of mettle that in truth I did not know I had, and finally I stirred a little soft into her bed. Then I dismounted. She was soothed by this, as was I. And despite a few sobs, she seemed no more troubled by my presence as does a copperhead sunning itself on a rooftop.

Thus contented, I sheathed my sparrow and re-cloaked myself in the Clothed Woman's garments before attempting to re-fix my love's garments as best I could, leaving her on the requited matrimonial bed. A piece of her rent pajamas I sequestered for myself, and there was no blood shed on it as I had been led by chattering Brothers to expect. The Lord be praised.

I then withdrew from the chambers, across the alleyway and into the coffeehouse's galley, and then into the celebratory hall where rested my cousin. I returned to his carcass. A cheerless patina had settled on him. In animals, I have noticed, there is much suffering that accompanies departure. Not so in man, but he smelled something awful, like a Missourian city with the plague.

Would that. Would that. Would that he had been a more resolute foil.

I removed the turban from my head—what a look I had had, enrobed in a Clothed Woman's cloak while wearing my cousin's crown!—and re-anointed him. For his final nighttime, I thought, he should have it.

Resolute or not, foil or not, watching him expire, giving him a name, I learned a way to need him, even to love him. And wasn't that what we sought from our relations? From our beloved? From our Lord? A love that found the strength to sustain us in the hereafter? For is He not also the One who Loves?

A single oil lamp guttered on an adjacent table. The other lanterns had spent their spartan supply, but not this one. I fled with this light, tiptoeing out of the hazy coffeehouse.

I returned my rank cloak to a washerwoman's line, and I shielded my eyes from the fresh-born sun. The Black Goat snored beside the holy well, and a rooster crowed from an unseen perch. I returned to my chambers atop the minaret— my wanderings unwitnessed, save for a phalanx of goats. I fell into an uncolored sleep, as one weary from his travels.

The next morning, I awoke to an ungodly scent: The sleeves of my tunic must have sopped up goat grease for they courted no small brigade of maggot suitors! I shook them athwart and quickly disrobed, secreting the prayer beads into my suitcase.

The lamp I had borrowed refused to unglow, and so on my way to the mosque, I dropped it into the well, which was unattended. But from that vantage, I could see why: Worshippers agitated outside the scene of the previous evening's festivities.

I approached them just as a bedraggled Brother burst from the coffeehouse. He wept openly, publicly, as if encouraging us to join his sorrow.

THE FINAL HOME

Faisal's funeral—would that I could forget it!

It was all too glorious an occasion. If they had asked me, which they did not, he should have been laid before us on the slab of an embalmer's table, and his heels tapped like a maple. Fluids and languages drained. Flesh eaten raw as salted afterbirth!

(Had they at least removed his tongue with a swift knife flick and buried it wrapped in muslin, then I would not have to hear him still. Am I the only one who hears him whisper as if his lips know the hairy contours of my ears? There is an angry weather in my head, and I am afraid that when there is finally thunder, it will burst. Then will I require bandages!)

I wish I had been strong enough to have built a pyre, a rectangle of intertwined birch, willow, and dry oak no more than five feet long, maybe a foot tall. I could have carried the wood myself, stripped the forest bare: With tools already blessed, my hands would have worked fast. Behind the coffeehouse, now the holy site of his expiration, was a patch of dry, sand-like dirt where I think was once a fireplace or black-top stove from a farm or church long-since quarried, fallen into disuse. On that open shore, I could have built a nice pyre.

Perhaps I would have needed help and hired a crew of miners with grit in their gums—for who else would have done it? The foreman, adjusting his cap, would have shouted, "Will this be enough sir? Are you sure? It's not very big. Is this really a man? Are we incinerating a goat?" With zealots, I have noticed, it takes no time to accomplish the largest of deeds.

I would, of course, have lit the pyre myself with a long match, the kind I have used to light tobacco or send firecrackers to Heaven to signal the end of the Fasting Month. I was not a scholar, but of all the unanswered questions of his death, this was the one I needed answered most: What color does a man of substance burn?

But this is all speculation and fanciful thinking. There is no truth in it anywhere. There was no embalmer's table, no pyre, no able-bodied men, no fireworks. There was no funeral as I had wished.

So much would have been gained if only I had acted quicker! Stolen and sequestered him from those God-fearing. Before they scoured his body in their plaintive way.

In the end, however, he did find his hole.

And it was all too convenient. Unfair of us to help. To put him wrapped into soil like a benign fruit, all too easy! (Burn instead, burn!) Let us hope that the tenderfoots never play the same games as the adults or one day there will be a plague of wriggling mounds in the Garden of Immortality—his graveyard, not my garden.

When we prepared his body for interment, I saw him fully unclothed, and the scale of his fraudulence was revealed. He courted many welts and blemishes! Many more than he admitted and many more than the poets have sung!

When the Brothers had finished washing him with a soap that smelled to me of a type of sweetwood, if bark can be said to have a flavor, and swathed him in a light muslin, I exacted my only revenge—a burdensome word for what was an effortless deed.

Once again, I found myself alone with him. This time, on a slab in the mosque's basement. From the pockets of my pressed tunic, I removed round stones that I had found the day I promised myself that I would brain him like a calf at the river market. I pulled apart the covering that encased what was his face. Saw the blood there pooled and dried, encrusting his eyes like those fat caterpillars. I may have laughed. I may have smiled. A smirk may have cracked across my face. His jaws opened. Three stones nested in the glass house that was once his mouth.

Shortly after, I returned outside. The imam, the Brothers, my teary-eyed love, Ms. A_____ and her father, my Auntie Maryam, the milling mass with their ravenous eyes none the wiser.

I wish I could say that from this point his processional was uneventful. That in my way, even if I was the only one to know, I was luminary. His carcass, I must admit, both revealed and upstaged my clandestine labors.

He refused to stay buried!

The Brothers carried him from the mosque's bathhouse on a wooden plank, which someone said was like a palanquin for a king or a queen. Each man positioned himself so that when one fell or stumbled another would quickly shoot up in his place. Seeing this cortège function together, weaving in and out of each other's path, reminded me of something animal or mechanical that I was sure I had never seen.

They took him in this funny manner to the Garden of Immortality, where the outsized imam lowered himself into the pit, muddying his vestments, which I could only assume he had worn for this day, where he was handed the body of my cousin who he then placed into a den of earth so uneven it was a shame to call it Kansan. Where Faisal proceeded to roll over from his side, to flat on his stomach.

At this point, the soiled priest, whose beard, a solemn grey, finally matched the elder Brown's in length, tried again to prop him on his shank so that he would face the proscribed direction, northeast I believed. And it was not long after interring him, that my cousin was exhumed. But no sound came from his mouth! His tongue lay still. Oppressed, for the moment, by my handicraft!

He was then, I was told for I did not go back inside, re-washed and re-wrapped. It was during this time, Faisal's second funeral of the day, that my stones were unearthed. They were given to my aunt for when next I saw them, they were in the palms of her furrowed hands. She was rolling them slowly, methodically, one over the other.

Auntie Maryam closed her fists and raised the stones above her head in much obvious, I would say ostentatious, delectation. If I was ever worried that these objects would be linked to my person, I did nothing to show it and stood as softly as I had been standing, at most crossing or perhaps uncrossing my unencumbered legs. Her face had shed its muddy-tea color until all that remained were two flyspecks on her cheeks. They hung beneath her sunken eyes like tears. Tears that would not fade but that were inscribed onto her.

In a raised voice, my aunt hailed these stones as a miracle as if she was a qualified judge. A final proof to those still in disbelief that her son could ever to something amount.

He had even in death, she proclaimed to the somber crowd, spoken his hard, heralding language. She wiped her face dry on the sleeve of the imam's cloak, who it seems had been the one to find my small bequest, and called the stones, "Faisal's prophetical geodes." She tied tight the tails of her headscarf beneath her chin as if preparing for battle. The Clothed Women did so too.

The three round stones that I found in the dry riverbed, the ones with which I intended only harm, sit encased in a box that any brazier would be proud of. They have to my knowledge been visited by Heads of State from as far away as Iowa.

Throughout, the Brothers were busy. New recruits, their mirrored caps glinting like tiaras, scurried about to excavate a new gravesite. In the heat, I found myself staring at them like a sun-drugged horse and was excused for not assisting because I was, as they said, in mourning.

Many did not look as a contraption dug Faisal a new hole, spewing spent fuel, streaking the white sky with black teeth marks. The churning hum drowned out a plangent sound that had by now made its way from wherever the source of sadness is to the mushrooms of my throat. I was always thankful that in a dialogue of noise, one's sorrow was often mistaken for machinery.

From this point, my memory wanes. I remember that he was wrapped, poised, ready to ascend. That rain came by way of handfuls of dirt. That we all took our turns, hurling country at his uncooperative corpse. That I aimed mainly for his head and his sparrow as I was certain he would have aimed at mine. That the dry russet dirt left dust on my hands. And with a clap, with a clap it was gone.

DEATH TO THE STRAWMAN

Would that our borders could constrain the telling of our tales!

I had thought that with my cousin safely, finally interred, the imam and my aunt would find me deserving of accolades and recognition, of the praise they had dispatched on him. Was I not a suitable replacement for an ascendant son? Had I not given that cousin boy a strong and fitting name with which to greet the Lord?

I had.

Instead, scrutiny found me! The Brothers held a mild suspicion against my person, which they enacted by sending a boy in ill-fitting trousers to pursue me as I discharged the few duties that were upon me burdened. Elements of our congregation also seemed to suspect me, as was their wont. That they could not know me, know my name, I had come to appreciate.

But what of those who would adhere to my honest and genuine and diminutive nature? Certainly, those who never spoke out against me at the time—my aunt, Bahira, Ms. A_____—certainly, they all were my mute accomplices!

After my cousin's interment and until at least the announcement of the impending birth of my son, a fog or a low-hanging cloud engulfed my aunt. Having outlived both of her offspring and perhaps one husband, she seemed to find little else in this world to consecrate—despite my unencumbered presence! She emerged infrequently from the mosque and courted a walking affliction that forced her to yaw and waddle. Not unlike my earlier disablement. The Lord be praised.

The partisanry was once again subjected to the commandments of the now graybeard imam, whose own paltry magic, such that he had it, seemed to expire with my cousin. But they did listen to him nevertheless, and it did seem to becalm the djinns that tormented them.

Like my aunt, my love Ms. A_____, who had on her wedding night become a widow, sequestered herself in her rusticated home. Her doughy father ever present. Although she abdicated the coffeehouse's stage, after the evening prayer when I would knead myself against the walls of her shack, my forlorn love serenaded me with a melody of sobbing and crying and what sounded like teeth-gnashing.

Would that I had had the courage to ask for her hand! Was it not customary for a brother to inherit his departed sibling's wives? Was not Faisal to me like a brother?

Would that he was.

I tucked the prayer beads I liberated from him beneath the collar of my tunic. They made no sound against my pigeon chest.

But even in Ms. A_____'s absence, I continued to frequent the smoldering coffeehouse where I shuttered my eyes and indulged in seasoning until the poet's voice transformed into hers and asked: *Oh F_____, did you know how we loved you?*

The table on which Faisal had rested his final rest had been at first sent-off and then returned to us covered in bronze! It transformed—into a useless thing that the worshipful gawked at, revered, and were saddened by. Our own Karbala on the Plains. A stop on a pilgrimage that enriched the Family man, who, like my aunt's once husband, had taken to selling baubles of a prayerful sort. Obscene was what it was. And, I was made to stare at that table where my cousin and I had tussled every time I haunted the coffeehouse!

Many mornings I awoke after spending the day sipping chicory and regarding the poets, sooty and slumped against my love's home, with my sparrow spent, a crow knotting strands of my hair. Vile bird!

But I was forgiven my appearance because I was, as they said, in mourning. The Lord be praised.

The Story of the Tongue, the fable by which the unfortunate incidents at my cousin's funeral became known, rushed from mouth-to-ear-to-mouth like in a tenderfoot's game! As if my departed-cousin-now-seated-in-Heaven's last act was to form mere stones from words.

Would that I had liberated his member instead of attempting to weigh it down!

Entranced by the tongue's tale, the disheveled arrived again into the forts that fortified our teeming rivers. Delegates, as my aunt had taken to calling them, as if we were being visited by temporary, out-of-State dignitaries, shouldered whatever belongings they could heft from whatever homes they had fled. The slight womenfolk stewarded the children, beating the unruly with blunt staves like filthy sheep shepherding filthier lambs. Clothed Women, not I, sprinkled them with rosewater, though I continued to brew the foul syrup.

The Delegates overwhelmed the Kansas Welcoming Committee, who abdicated their astringent-dousing regimen to let the migrants fester and threaten to infect us with their travelling maladies! Why was it that the wretched, the destitute, the enfeebled, the pitiable, and the ugly were always in need of saving! Why not those Hereford-fattened men of the central plains who smelled of tobacco flower even at a distance? Why was it that the prosperous and the comely never needed salvation?

With the arrival of the Delegates, tales of my cousin spread through the camp like the wildfires and whirlwinds that from time-to-time engulfed our prairies. There were rumors of the tame sort: He could heal the lame. Of the untrue variety: He was born of no earthly father. The mystical: Stones flew from his mouth when he spoke. The mundane: His form appeared on springy cornbreads, and His profile etched into fry breads.

Enterprising Brothers profited on this latter rumor and manufactured a hearth toaster that imprinted my cousin's wide-smiling face onto a variety of wheat and corn products in a converted, or reverted if you prefer, slaughterhouse to the west of the mosque. They called it Auntie Maryam's Bread of Piety and delivered it to the bazaar and to fairs throughout the State.

Would that I had a square with me now. One unengraved with my cousin's likenesses!

With the influx of these clumsy migrants, I was decreed a new task—the harvesting of parts. An eruption from the forest would mar the tranquility: not Missourians nor miners, but land torpedoes planted by the Browns that disassembled a misguided or unwarned Delegate.

You may ask: Were the Browns faulted for seeding this bloodthirsty fruit? I may answer: Was the Lord faulted when the wild wind uprooted saplings that then speared adherents?

Into my wheelbarrow, I harvested bits of a lost pilgrim from the trees as if reassembling a string puppet. Trinkets I removed and collected, buckles, rings, false teeth, buttons of bone or ivory, before wheeling the char to the boneyard. With the tip of the laden barrow, I dumped the remains into The Tomb of the Unknown Pilgrim, which the Brothers had dug just paces from the vault that held my cousin! At the waning of each moon, the imam took to the tomb and read a prayer over the mass grave so that the souls of the departed would find true and speedy course on a flaming chariot to the Heavens above.

To Him we belong, I thought.

So you see, save for the diminutive Brother's fervent interest in my wanderings—what did he scrawl in that journal of his?—little changed for me with the departure of my cousin. My once gruesome task, the slaughtering of beasts, replaced by another no less gruesome task, the harvesting of parts.

But, I was given no fresh appellations that I knew of. May the Lord be praised!

Precipitated by the influx of Delegates, the Brothers oversaw the construction of new habitations—the Kansas Plains Authority, I think that's what they termed the project—a system infallible save for the general lethargy and incompetence chiseled in by the sun. But several seasons passed before we required the fabrication of another grove of outhouses. By then, tenements sprawled from the mosque to the dry riverbed, from the forest to the trail. We were overrun was what we were!

I recall well the day the outhouses were to be completed for it was nearly the day I received the best news that I ever had in my short and wonderous and woeful life. And it will come as no surprise to you that this news was the impending birth of my child!

The day began as such: I was alerted to the presence of a decaying pilgrim, or so I thought, by a clutch of buzzards circling over the forest—the Lord's glorious creatures assisted my humble form! I scraped gore from out my wheelbarrow and drove it into the timberland, weaving to-and-fro as if being pursued by a mob of Delegates from whom I had thieved a prized calf. My shovel rasped against the bucket as I skittered along, and the diminutive Brother followed me to the forest's edge and then relented, afraid of the booby-traps. But I knew it well enough to know that land torpedoes, once discharged, held no other charm.

Bereft of leaves, the timber raked the cloudless vault. I tracked the carrion-eaters to the devastated site. Entrails in bilious purples littered the scene like a shredded curtain of meat. It was not a man but a lean deer that had been ripped apart. Hindquarters dangled from a low branch, while the slender head nuzzled into the earth.

This deer was beyond repair, and my first thought was that

we would be eating stringy venison that night. I circumambu-
lated the strewn animal, but meat was not salvageable from its
rawboned remains. Steam rose, and as I knelt to the muzzle, I
saw that a breath huffed from the not venison.

I cleared the animal's nostrils and saw there was a timid
life in it, imploring me to assist with its dispatch. I stroked
the beast's head and kissed a blanched spot on its pelt. Its ear
twitched. I took this as a good sign.

There there now.

I grabbed the shovel and aligned the spade with the neck.
I did what I had been trained to do and acted as a pure agent
of the Lord, cleaving the animal's spirit from its body as I did
its head. On my downward stroke, the hindquarters of the
beast kicked in the tree, and the pulpy assembly crashed down.
In a moment, I recognized that I was unscathed, but my feet
were garlanded in the animal's bowels. I unwound the char and
fought back nausea from the churning stench.

My second stroke did the final renting. I was certain that
the Lord's work had never come to anyone as simply as it did
for me that morning.

The head I placed in the barrow, and it seemed to stare at
me with those wide, ladylike eyes as if I was responsible for its
habitation. And so with the 'V' of my fingers, I shut them.

Carrion-eaters crashed nearby, and I let nature, if indeed
buzzards are of the Lord and not born in the eternal fires, run
its course. I skinned the deer's face and donated the flesh to
those creatures. As I have said, I was generous, kind, and a
whole slew of other benedictions.

Then, I took the skull to the well and rinsed it like it was
the dislodged heart of a holy man. I rested the skull on a step
at the base of my tower. Its grin seemed monstrous to me, and
I hoped it would act as a fright to any who would enter. Would
that I had had a snarling mongrel to protect me.

(I admit here that at times an additional step did return on my ascent or even descent in the minaret. Iblis, I was certain, worried the hearts of geometricists the worst or perhaps the best.)

I then drove my barrow onto the clearing in which the Brothers were erecting the outhouses. In not a moment, I recognized the place as both the site of my parent's or perhaps parents' grave marker and of my own Garden of Immortality. Both had been uprooted and discarded as if neither held any ability to enchant!

I found the manufactured grave marker and ran my fingers across it before kissing them in blessing. A breeze whipped through the clearing, followed by a bomb bursting. Missourians! I spat into the dust. There was a hiss in the dry grass, but I witnessed nothing vexing.

Because I was no longer, as they said, in mourning, I assisted the Brothers as we marshalled planks and hammered nails into the supports like at a barn raising. I procured a handsaw and cut openings into the outhouse platform and beneath them placed tin pails like the ones we used to harvest goat's blood. Sprinkling copperas, I spat the grime from out my mouth. A pyramid of corncobs awaited the happy evacuators.

My aunt waddled over to join us in the labors, her Women unpresent. Though I protested, with a spade she cleaved twain my parent's or perhaps parents' putative grave marker, calling it a talisman. Perhaps she had seen my earlier devotion, I thought, and sought to curtail the practice. She tossed the splintered wood into the pile of scrap that held my harvested seasoning. She made no mention of her supposed sister or her supposed brother.

Perhaps now, I thought, I might ask: What have you heard of my mother? My father? I leaned forward to not miss her reply. Those stout beads I had annexed from my cousin tugged at my scruff.

Auntie Maryam rested her spade and snatched with her ashen hands at a stubborn scrub grass. The roots dangled as she succeeded in disgorging it. Leached of color and it seemed to me courting a chill, she tossed the creepers into the pile of detritus to attend to me.

I could not recall in her the woman who had once blocked out the sun. Who had once enveloped me. Who had once given us hope. She had moldered and enfeebled. Perhaps I too had moldered. Perhaps now was the moldering time. Oh, hideous rot of life!

With tearless eyes she gritted out, "Your mother was my sister. One of my sisters. I do not recall when she left us. She had written to us once. And your father was a man who…"

As I drew nearer, Auntie Maryam cut short her sermon.

"Where did you get these, boy?" she snapped, snatching at the beads, which had slipped from under my shirt.

I coughed once or twice. I stared into her scary face with dumb wonderment as the dirt whipped us. I could not get the words out. I could not recall for her from whose neck they had been purchased—for so long had I felt that they were mine.

"Where, boy?" she demanded, bouncing the beads in her hand. A licorice scent alighted on her breath. Her barbed fingers scraped my throat.

"I have been searching for these," she revealed. "Bahira too. How did you come upon them?" Her tone softened as she clenched her palm around the strand. "They were to be buried with your cousin."

Delegates and Brothers, perturbed by the scene, clucked in disapproval. Their glances lingered on my form and away from their zealous tasks. On my form, and then away.

Maryam grasped me by the shoulders and spun me around. Although unencumbered, my feeble appendages were unused to such vigorous attention, and I tumbled to the ground.

The Brothers with their caps and matted beards, their grubby teeth, made their way to us, crowding in, blocking out the sun. At that moment, I could only hope that the Lord would find a way to safeguard His namesake!

And He did! The storm before the calm! Safeguarded by my own son! In sooth, he is a luckless child, a soon to be fatherless child, but he saved me that lamentable and promising afternoon!

As my aunt and the Brothers menaced in their manner, that plump Family man, Ms. A_____'s father, bullied through the gang. As was his wont, he cried for my aunt in a peal of anguished joy.

Maryam's fingers slipped the beads from my neck, nicking my precious flesh and drawing blood, as the Family man compelled her in a celebratory manner towards her once daughter-in-law's chambers. The Brothers skittered after, save for that one in ill-fitting trousers who scribbled furiously in his journal.

And I, I fled. I fled back to the minaret.

But at least this much I knew: I had had a mother. She was my aunt's sister. I had had a father. My history for which I bartered my safety. For this was the sorrowful sum of familial warfare.

Practitioners of the vocation of midwifery had been anointed with the honorific Talib after the woman who had aided my young aunt, and one such Talib, whether native or Delegate I was uncertain, had pronounced Ms. A_____ gravid.

While I was being interrogated by my aunt in the outhouse grove, a Talib informed that gluttonous proprietor of his daughter's condition, and he then fetched my aunt to celebrate the pronouncement, though I was not told at the time. Word of the imminent offspring would reach me a day later by blathering Delegates as I disbudded kids.

As you have witnessed, elation was not a sentiment I was accustomed to courting. It was not an emotion that I had ever companioned. So, I was not elated or joyful when I overheard of the miraculous child of our Redeemer.

No, instead I was thankful. I was understanding. I was, as I have mentioned, not a scholar, but I was capable of understanding, of reasoning that the birth of a child attributed to my cousin the Savior would be met with no animosity from the faithful—and instead with a type of joy.

But was I happy?

And here be it revealed: I knew not that one could weep in happiness until the day I learned of Ms. A_____'s pregnancy, but that was what I did. Alone in a pen as I sawed horns off beasts, I wept. And I wept. And I was certain that my tears soothed the animals' raw scalps just as they did my own face.

But joy, that inconsequential sentiment, was the one my aunt and the triumvirate that now leads us—I include the Family man in this oligarchy because he will be like a grandfather to my child—thought to promote. There were joyful proclamations, joyous celebrations, and even a joyless invocation preached in the coffeehouse for my unborn son, steps from where he was conceived! But I was not asked to participate in the ceremony because I was, as they said, in a state of elation.

It seemed that the distraction created by Ms. A_____'s condition had unburdened the scrutiny that had been placed upon me from certain sectors of our populace—their attention spans known for their lack of longevity! And perhaps it was this joy that allowed my aunt to forgive my pilfering of my cousin's beads? For after all, as I eventually would concede to her, had I not found them in the coffeehouse unattended by any living soul? The Lord be praised!

Ms. A_____ had, I gleaned from chattering Brothers, divulged to no person that she was heavy until the biliousness compelled her. And for her part, she remained my resolute accomplice. I forgave her for courting the fantasy that the child was my cousin's. I was certain that when her cheerless eyes failed to meet mine as we lurched past each other in the courtyard of the holy well, our hushed conspiracy strengthened. Our

parentage fortified itself against the insults and depredations
that were hurled at the husbandless, the wifeless, the urchins.
The parts of families.

Here be it asked: How did you know at the time that she
would bear you a son, if the child was awaited and not a formed
thing, yet a clot of clay?

To this I can only answer that I knew. That fathers know.
That the Lord provided first-born sons to the faithful. For did
not Ibrahim have an Ismail?

My son. Not my cousin's but my son. Even if at the time
I was the only one to know that he was a son and to acknowl-
edge that he was mine.

Sometime after we raised the outhouses, after Ms. A_____'s
father had apprised my aunt of her incipient heir, the imam
offered to bless the new grove. I crept into the mosque as
the Brothers prepared for the service. Droplets of light spilled
across the tile. It created a dizzying effect that was compounded
by the growing numbers of our worshippers. I had never gotten
accustomed to the mosque like this—for so long had I been
used to its desolation!

The journaling diminutive Brother, that spy, kept close
by me. But he was accompanied by others, as if the Brothers
spread their seeds like springtime dandelions! I asked this boy's
name, but he scurried away, unaccustomed to being addressed,
I thought. Not unlike myself!

The imam's office was depopulated, and so I entered. A
collection of armaments blockaded the bookshelves, and the
priest had reimagined a crate of rifles as a dressing table. But
across Bahira's burnished desk, a peculiar map confronted me:
It was a projection of our State with the northeastern shores
linearized.

I traced the borders on the puckered vellum. From the

Kawsmouth north past St. Joseph, and then west along a parallel, former Missouri lands had been annexed so that our Country formed a true rectangle!

It was an awesome sight. Inspiring. A sensation burned in me—akin to the one I had when I tamed the martyred Fanatic's steed! Honor, perhaps.

The rectangle: a figure rivaled only by the holy square for its clarity, for its virtue. Unlike the deviant circle with its siren curves, the square and the rectangle were humble, unadulterated. *For the Lord loves a perfect symmetry.*

Across the top of Bahira's map, a banner proclaimed: *"ad Allah per asperum."* A smile may have bloomed across my face. Or a tear shed. A knot may have stoppered my throat.

The imam entered his office and snatched a gnarled chewing stick that rested in a puddle of drool atop the parchment. His beard flashed white, regaining its old magic for the moment and registering my excitement at the map's promise.

"Very soon!" he bleated, and he continued into the prayer hall.

I found a magnifier that revealed smaller rectangles set into our State's boundaries and larger ones carved into our neighbors'. In one of the new renderings, parts of eastern Colorado, our westerly adversary, reverted to Kansan suzerainty! (These lands, I had been told by the elder Brown, were once allocated to our Country but never relinquished when that State was formed. But certainly, it seemed, that oversight was to be corrected in the blood and treasure of the Coloradoans!)

Unaccustomed to such a prideful feeling, I jigged—jigged!—my way into the prayer hall after the imam. Brothers of a soldierly sort trailed behind, and one obstructed me as I tried to enter. Then yet another, a hulking sort wearing darkened lenses indoors for a reason I could not appreciate, slapped the obstructionist, and I was granted admission.

These were the men that I was to fear. The men Missourians

were to fear. I would later come to know this bespectacled man as my captor, but he was not that yet.

In the prayer hall, Brothers handed out pamphlets and recruited young, feather-faced Delegates to their ranks with promises of glory, redemption, revenge. They hailed the Lord above and my cousin in the same blaspheming, in my humble opinion, breath. They chanted the poems of our tribe: the Song of the Battle of the Ditch, the Story of the Tongue, the Healing of the Cripple. A festive occasion it was if that was your notion of festivity.

One Brother, who was bereft of hair but wore a trim beard tinted a burnt orange in imitation of the imam's magic, had assumed my duties and replaced our old rugs and their tame embroideries of the Cube with Kansan prayer flags: rectangles of dyed and woven cotton that were nearly the hue of the clear, untrammeled sky, but darker, more menacing. If pigments can be said to threaten. The words, *"ad Allah per aspera"* were scripted in a blonde thread across the top.

The modest prayer hall transformed with this handiwork: Some saw a patchwork sea that rippled underfoot. Others, the vault of the Heavens.

I witnessed nothing less than the usurpation of a proven deity for the exaltation of a manufactured Redeemer who could or would not—here be it said—safekeep himself from the perfidy of my calloused hands!

Atop this "Kansan Sea," as many had taken to calling it, and before a clutch of Brothers rested a bale and a giant costume of straw. It was a suit banded with twine the likes of which I had not seen since the detachment had left to fight the Missourians at the Ditch. As you know from the poetry, the poor fellow who had first slipped on a costume such as this one had perished in that battle, and I could not stomach the sight of another one.

Like womenfolk weaving, Brothers plaited the stalks into

bindings and gathered it into the appendages. There was a slit in the back, large enough for someone or someones to slip into. A prophetical uniform to wear over our skin.

Bahira wore a bandolier that read "Imam," and he climbed into the costume. What this theater was that he was enacting I was unsure, but I trailed him to the outhouse grove dutifully, dependably. The Brother with darkened lenses hefted a can of kerosene that slapped against his thigh as we ambled down the well-trodden path to the site of my former Garden.

Our procession joined a crowd that had assembled in the shrubbery near the outhouses. They were an uninspiring lot, chatting in a gaggle of tongues, and they parted as a willow did for an axe when the strawman approached. Brothers assisted the imam as he then slipped off the costume that he had just put on! My aunt was unpresent, though the Women represented her and trilled as was their wont.

The Brother with the kerosene snaked through the crowd and hoisted the can above his head. It reflected sunlight like a beacon aflame. He doused the straw costume, before the imam stepped forward and stuttered, "Today, being that it is midday, we welcome you to these thrones. The Lord has provided. Let no Delegate nor Partisan nor citizen go unevacuated!"

A cheer—"God is Great"—arose from the Brothers, but the others held their ovation and awaited the conflagration.

Like he did at the Tomb of the Unknown Pilgrim, Bahira recited the prayer for the dead, *To Him we shall return*, over the strawman costume and then was handed a match. He tried to light it against the outhouse walls, failing thrice before it caught in his cupped hands. He dropped the lucifer onto the costume and fled into the crowd.

The strawman took the flame and was engulfed. There was in this inanimate thing no flailing of the arms, no running in circles as I thought there should have been. Instead, smoke rose in a spire and sullied the otherwise vacant sky. We watched as the crackling figure shrunk before us to cries of "Sunflower State zindabad!" and "God is Great!"

I returned to my tower where I perched on the lowest steps—one, two—and stroked the skull I had liberated from the dismantled deer. I could not fathom why in these not-so-lean times one would waste lucifers on pageantry? Or even why one would introduce said pageantry to our otherwise prosaic practices? Why the innovations? Wasn't our doctrine despoiled enough by my cousin's magic? Would that it was.

But then, I ciphered an answer. For what inspired a timid and stupid Partisanry more than spectacle? What emboldened even the most destitute of Delegate to take up arms against his neighbors? What was man's earliest tongue?

Fire, that was what. In every and all its forms. Fire, reasonably, reliably. Even the Zarathushtrans had sussed this much!

I could not be certain that this trickery was my aunt's handicraft, but her unpresence at the occasion was remarkable. Bahira himself, in my estimation, had no ability to entrance on his own! How far we had come from that day when the Jay-hawker Fanatics asked—no! begged!—us for assistance. When that meek imam fled from his chambers rather than press his flock into proper service.

But herein a great conflict vexed me. The cause, no doubt, was a worthy one: The occupiers, those vile long-haired wrecks whose handiwork could only be avenged, had to be exterminated! They had to be shown the folly of their ways with sharp instruments—this much was certain.

But I had to wonder: Did blood shed in the name of liberty stain its practice? Perhaps it did not?

For is He not also the One Who Victoriously Prevailed over His Enemies and Punished Them for their Sins?

That evening, the bewilderment of the day's events compelled me to seek out a comforting thing. So, I set out to recover my parent's or perhaps parents' grave marker from where I had last seen it—in the pile of detritus beside the new outhouse grove.

I trekked back to the freshly blessed outhouses and retrieved the pieces of the broken totem from where it had been tossed with the scrap and my seasoning into the straw-man's pyre. In my hands, the marker turned to ash, but the fire, like a lamp I once had owned, still smoldered.

I came to a solution that would for me forever satiate my unrelenting mind and its need for investigations!

I threw myself into the embers of the fire like a weeping sati. As did a one-armed doctor who had lost his brother to plague!

And because I knew where the heat hid, I dove to the deepest part!

But it was like most of my rebellions, a weak one, and like the stone of my tower, I was unable to catch fire. I succeeded only in sooting myself and extinguishing the flame.

As I choked on the ash of the strawman's and my parent's or perhaps parents' pyre, I feared that my sojourn at the mosque had come to its anticipated and foreseen conclusion since I was deposited here that sweltering morning long ago.

PASTOR GARRETT'S BOOTS

Between the mistrust of vindictive Brothers, the disregard of my person by my aunt and the increasing innovations of the imam to our worship, I had to quit the mosque. An urchin was forced to flee his home, such that it was, leave his love and his nascent son, and attempt to cross a border! To tramp onto a foreign soil! To resign—no, to reassign!—himself to the mercy of the Coloradoans.

Would that I had made it to the summit of a Great Peak, where country relents and transforms into Heavens! The Lord be praised!

After my attempted immolation at the outhouse grove, Brothers besieged me. I was not certain why, other than that they perceived me as a threat to their order, their fealty to the imam's innovations. The Brother in darkened lenses mostly admitted as much to me one night. It was after he apprehended me contorting myself outside Ms. A_____'s shack.

But imagine that—my humble form the source of their consternation! The Brothers sent tenderfoots in droves to shadow my sure steps. The little menaces, their numbers unceasing, sprung from behind the mosque's walls, beneath coffeehouse tables, and from around the well when I fetched water! They ascended the innumerable steps of my tower and ransacked my chambers. To harry and harass!

In truth, they absconded with a rat's harvest, but they gouged a blade into my deer skull and split it in half! Because sloth is infectious, they failed to molest the tarp that secreted my powder keg, and so it remained unused, but unforgotten!

These Brothers, as they threatened to do with the few non-Brothers, non-Partisans and non-believers who refused to leave the good land on which they were raised and immigrate into loathed Missouri, false Arkansas, dust-ridden Oklahoma, or another uninhabitable land, these Brothers would press for my tongue after relieving my body from the sweet burden of its head—I was no soothsayer, but of this I had become certain!

My final night as a civilian in the mosque, while suppli-cants supplicated, I readied for my departure. On a pallet, I laid out the trappings: bladders of well-water, goat jerky, hardtack, oatcake, tobacco and papers, a match box, deer teeth, a map scrawled by a Brown son, Ms. A_____'s ripped wedding trouser, pure white tunics—the kind favored by the Brothers themselves (I knew the meaning of the word subterfuge and it was conformity)—and the blade I had excised from the deer skull. I bundled these provisions into a gale blanket and lashed it to a branch of willow. Over the years, I have become adept at only a few things, most of them custodial or sanguinary in nature, but I can deftly denude branches of willow leaves.

I set the pack on the grit floor and hoisted onto my lap my aunt's treasured and illuminated Holy Book. On a foray into the imam's office for the letter marked K.U.D. that had delivered me to this bereft and inhospitable place, I had found and appropriated her prized possession. The book had a reassuring heft, all significant works announced as such by their carriage, and I parted the pages. I could not appraise the ancient script, but I saw the turbaned riders, mustaches fili-greed coal black, who buried their spurs into elephants that were colored blue as songbird eggs. They charged across a desert expanse. The beasts trickled crimson where pierced.

The riders, with protruding noses and flat eyes, resembled a cavalry of Faisals.

In the illustration, inky birds ripped through the skies above the elephant-riders and carried stones in their beaks. It made for a horrifying scene even before I flipped to the familiar slaughter on the next page.

Words that attested to the might of the Almighty were forged in a faded gold ink beneath the gory images. Or so I surmised. From what I had learned in the mosque, I knew at least that the Lord needed attesting to. For He is the One Who Deserves to be Praised!

The page that had been torn by the shepherd's son fell from the book and slipped into my grasp. It retained creases from the plump Family man's travels, and I re-folded it and tucked the page into my tunic. It sorrowed me that I could not bring the meaty book on my journey. Perhaps it would find its way back to my aunt, I thought.

I rested the tome on the pallet and scanned my minaret. Undisturbed, the blasting powder retained its noxious authority. I recognized that I no longer possessed the one item with which I had arrived at the mosque: my leg braces. They sat glistening in a reliquary in Topeka as testament to my cousin's revivalism.

Children squealed, and I shuffled to the window. Draped in their mourning whites, my glorious aunt and her Women led the Delegates' brood in prayer in the mosque's gravel lot. Having lost both of her offspring, my aunt tended to those of the recent arrivals. The gristly brats, many of them clothed in my cousin's threadbare cast-offs, mimicked Auntie Maryam as the parishioners did the imam. Their yelps rode the whorls of rising spring air as the prayers wound down.

In unison the worshippers whispered right, left to the angels on their shoulders. Their mumblings were audible as high up as my tower and as far away, I liked to think, as Jefferson City, where it worried the hearts of that suspect tribe.

Evening came bruising through the sky. With my Jupiter finger, I traced the setting sun.

It was the first prayer I had missed since his ascension.

It did seem appropriate enough an occasion.

The worshipful minions caromed out of the mosque, herded their ticklish brood, nodded solemnly to my aunt— several must have said deferential, neighborly words to her and her companions—and then settled into the tents, shacks, shanties, sheds, huts and other hastily-built shelters that sufficed for their dirt-floored homes. Would that I had set flame to that village when I had a chance.

With this group, Ms. A_____ emerged from the mosque. I thought that this would be my last chance to see her, and so I committed my mind to chronicling her movements with the vigor of those spies sent to shadow me! She was dressed in white like my aunt, and belly protruding, she wobbled into the courtyard. Delegates let her pass, and despite her funereal colors, she seemed unperturbed. No, she seemed gentle, easy as if hopeful. She and my aunt exchanged words and tendernesses before Maryam stroked her face. Then Ms. A_____ seemed to glide across the grounds and into her rusticated home.

I wept. In my chambers, I wept openly. I wept for the future I would not have with this love. With my son.

And I wept again—out of happiness! For the world my son would inherit. A world in which he had Ms. A_____ for a mother and a well from which to sip. A well that his true father had named. A world in which asylum was not a thing that the faithful had to pursue but was ever-present—a spiritual, imma-terial tenement.

And of course, a world that would rid itself of Missouri-ans. *Never think that the Lord is unaware of what the wrongdoers do*, I thought.

I awaited moonrise and plotted my course to the transverse road—the thoroughfare used to drive cattle from the western cantons of our State to the eastern markets. To mask the familiar contrivance of my face, I pulled the blade from my pack and denuded myself. A charcoal wool clumped atop my aunt's illustrated Holy Book. My face feminized, I felt scraped, descaled, born anew into the savage world.

"I am content with the Lord's protection," to myself I whispered. The words failed to placate me.

As was their nightly duty, two Clothed Women shut the mosque's gates against the panhandlers who hunkered outside. The rifle-toting sluggards who called themselves sentries would soon be asleep. Never underestimate the sloth of men who believe their sect victorious.

In the world outside my window, fruit bats quivered and shrieked, which to this day is for me a sound at once haunting and heartwarming.

I knew it was time.

I recall those final moments: excitement, anxiety, the drumming inside me drowning out the silver-tongued cacophony of the bats. I brushed stray whiskers off my person and the Book, tucked the works beneath my straw pallet, knotted the ropes of my sandals, snatched up my pack, laid a hand flat against the whitewashed walls, picked at a bubble of paint with a fingernail and forced my way out the bedroom door, which squealed on its castings. As I decamped from the room that I had inhabited since I was left here by the drover, I did not look back. Colorado—beautiful, bountiful Colorado—had consumed me! Where the good Lord blessed the mountaintops with snowfall year-round!

I spun down the minaret's staircase. The extra step had reappeared. Iblis, it seemed, was near to me this night. I crunched onto the gravel lot, into the buzzing air. Accustomed to the staleness of my tower and to my self-made scents, I inhaled the marrowy twilight and choked on a gnat.

ad Allah per aspera embroidered prayer rugs furled and unfurled in the lot. The disembodied palms of those seeking alms rummaged along the bars of the front gates. My fingers clenched around the drooping stick of my bundle.

Auntie Maryam was aping the one and true Redeemer, that was to say she was unseen. In all likelihood, she was confer-ring with the imam in his goatskin-adorned office, kneeling over a topographic map, wangling a rectangle over the borders, measuring, re-drawing, re-measuring.

As once I had, Brothers lazed in the beds of wagons. They insulated themselves with camel-brown shawls, not dissimi-lar to the one in which I was enrobed. A fearlessness roared through me as I craved to sneak up, bludgeon these goons in a raw-fisted fury and then steal a wagon. The craving quickly dissipated and left an ache in my hands, my chest. As I have already noted, I was not that sort of beast. Would that I was.

Somewhere, a goat roasted on a spit.

In truth, I was exhausted from the day's chores, which I performed, unasked, with a vigor that I had not mustered in previous efforts: sweeping and mopping, dusting, scouring, scraping, polishing, wiping—the general sanctifying that a mosque needed when it was visited daily by a hungry hoard of sorry, squalid, trashy, ugly, unworthy, wretched worshippers.

I did, however, not visit the coffeehouse. But I deposited a deer's tooth at Ms. A_____'s doorway so that she would have a thing by which to remember me. I had hoped that when my son was ready, she would deliver it to him and instruct him in the ways of his right and true father.

Tired as I was, the fear of being soon beheaded and having my tongue ripped out, or in some order thereof, spurred on my weary frame. Fear a strong motivator even for the gener-ally unmotivated.

To make it to the transverse trail, I would have to scoot unseen across the encampment. In addition to balding my face,

I needed a disguise, a subterfuge true and unerring. This was Faisal's domain, subterfuge. In the clotted sky above, the light between the streaming clouds, the moon and the setting sun begat his solemn face, speckled with downy beard and jaundiced with bile. My hands instinctively clutched his throat. I shook the specter away.

The wind dined on my shorn face as I scraped into the slumbering municipality, seeking a Clothed Woman's cloak. My possibles pack sheared through the brush. The air blistered with oil fires from the tenements, but at least there was no palpable rain. My route deserted by men, beast, the Lord's weather.

How monstrous the Delegates' camp had become never failed to dispirit me. The disorder in their old lands contained by Brothers acting as planners, designers, draftsmen, engineers, and unschooled architects, who accounted for the exacting dilapidations that were the worshippers' homes. This garrison of shacks gave me confidence that if it were necessary, I could erect a habitation on my own in the hinterland of the Kansan west.

A bazaar choked the center of the village and shanties radiated out in spokes. Walking paths furrowed throughout. One rut noosed its way around the mosque. Others ended at the murky well, the washerwomen's clotheslines, or the row of rank outhouses erected in the brush clearing.

Since my failed attempt at self-immolation, I hadn't returned to the outhouses to pay my mother or father her or his or their respects. And so there I paused, and thankfully, they were unoccupied and smelled only of pale wood. I sat in the center of the enclosure, cross-legged in the trodden earth. Mice jagged through the scrub, and it seemed as if the stunted bushes danced of their own volition.

Surrounded, I felt like a child in the palm of a comforting colossus. The outhouses: tented and towering fingers. Though I was not overcome by a feeling I could call visceral, I imagined this to be the place that I had before placed tributes on long journeys. I dug my heels into the land as I did my hands. The scorched country soothed my palms. The wind kicked through the brush, ruffling my trappings. I shaded my face and blinked away grains that teared my eyes.

Dislodged from a washer line, a Clothed Women's shroud blanketed an outhouse and barked in the wind. And so once again, I donned the matronly garb before deploying the Brown man's sons' map as a guide. I inaugurated my westward trek with an exhaled prayer, "In the name of the Almighty, Gracious and Merciful Lord," and in no time found the dry riverbed that corralled our compound. Soon enough, I was onto the transverse throughway, which at this rude hour was perturbed only by vermin, but not by man or beefs.

As morning threatened, the sky began to blaze. I required a berth, a concealed one, and so with my meager hands, I dug a ditch in the wet soil beside the throughway. I rolled into it, set my pack atop me, and buried myself as best I could so as not to be seen. The ruse worked! I went unmolested and slumbered in this tomb throughout the day until night again fell. Then, I hoisted myself out, shook off country, and micturated. The pit had consumed my sandals, and there they remain should you seek a thing by which to remember me. It was now my season for pilgrimage, my hijra.

To get to Colorado, I tramped across our land like an unshod ascetic, enshrouded in the tatters of a Clothed Women's cloak. I kept sight of the transverse but sought copses when I could. The sodden country calmed my abused soles, and the friendly and becalming waves of prairie grasses entranced my weary spirit.

After devouring my provisions in a frenzied feast, I chomped insects, wild grapes and berries, worms, trapped an enfeebled bushy-tailed squirrel, and refilled my gourd from the creeks that baptized this State. Would that that Black Goat carted for me barrels!

And once I did witness them: The Terrorists! The Irregulars! The Missourians!

The story was as follows: I had encountered a meadow path and witnessing no herd or cattlemen thought to follow it into a shrouded forest. Although I could descry no bats, what a pleasure it was to discover a woodland so similar to the one near the minaret!

But my ardor soon abated as a scent like soured milk accosted me! Then I heard a bleating and recalled our familiar herd. I thought to ambush these wandering beasts and slit their throats, tasks at which I was adept. I deployed furtive measures, maneuvering from tree to tree, circumventing fallen branches lest a careless footfall scatter the quarry.

As I arrived, the bleating transformed into what might be called speech: A pair of grizzled long-hairs dismembered a pack animal of a sort and yelped at each other. Could one even call this yapping language? It summoned in my memory a derelict version of that tongue in which my cousin and the imam preached. But I suspected that even Brown the elder would find hardship parsing the dialogue between these patriarchs.

Their rifles were planted in front of them like flag posts and from one draped a battered triband flag.

I thought on the seasoned Fanatics who had beseeched Bahira for assistance in the pre-Delegate days, in the idle time before we suffered the sensations of my cousin and my aunt. A bolt-action in my arms was prudent to have on this journey, and as Missourians were known cowards, the advantage in any altercation with these men was mine—undoubtedly. Plus, I had the Lord's name, and He would act to safeguard my person from these non-believers.

And so with memories of the Fanatics and the Browns, I rushed to the rifles and they to me. And I scored the decorated instrument!

"Missourians," I roared, "I bring you slaughter!"

I leveled the weapon at these Sarah-loving Terrorists, although the flag drooped below the barrel as if I were a celebrated member of their tribe. Call me Quantrill, if you must!

"Little shalt thou laugh and much shalt thou weep," I hollered, mimicking a line from a sermon I had heard my cousin give.

The men peered from between the shanks of the camel they had been dismantling. You couldn't see their eyes from the gore on their faces. One raised his arms in surrender, as I had expected, exposing his tobacco-stained teeth. And the other, after glancing my way, returned to butchery.

We remained in this pose until the butcher carved a hunk from the shank and presented it to me. He had not known it, but he aped the machinations of my counterfeit father Bahira so many years before! And indeed, of myself—the Cripple Butcher of Kansas!

Unsure of this Missourian deception, but certain of my appetite, I inched toward his outstretched appendage with the rifle raised. I snatched the meat from him and fled with the weapon and my pack.

I huffed from the abominable scene until I confronted a clearing in which to raise a fire and roast the meat. The rifle was cumbersome and, like my love Ms. A____, stouter than I had suspected. After ravaging the tough meat, I slung the bolt open on the instrument. To my consternation, it was barren. I had been no more than a sluggard levelling it at those Bushwhackers and had done them a service by absconding with this hefty impotence! I buried the weapon right then and there to sequester it from those carrying munitions.

Rain came by way of the vault, and I scattered back into the forest until I encountered what I thought was a ghastly and haggard house: slats failing, windows sagging. There was a breach in the crown of this habitation, but like he had with Hajar and Ismail in the uncultivated valley, the Lord had provided!

I scaled a trampled fence and across a field of stones that

fractured underfoot like skullcaps. But a padlocked doorway forestalled my admission.

Invited by the windows that framed the entrance, I wrapped my hand in my cloak, smashed a pane, and crawled inside to find not a habitation for man, but one for the Lord—for what I had entered was a decrepit church! The pews were befouled, but what was more disconcerting: The belfry had crashed inside, and the bell had clobbered a pastor. A collar that read Garrett choked his still smirking skeleton. I shooed away varmints that had nested in his sand-colored hair, which despite the lack of a spirit still retained its hue. The pastor's remains recalled those of an animal thing that I was sure I had never seen.

In a gulp, I emptied my gourd and set it to refill under a trickle of rainwater.

With my sage, unmoving companion, I rested in this counterfeit ossuary, harvesting what I could from the creepers, the vermin, and the vegetation that had taken up worship. Fruit bats shrieked and roosted in an oak outside. That I had escaped one so-called house of worship for the dispiriting confines of another was not lost on me. Though the bats, they were reassuring!

Was our land so wrecked by conflagrations that sanctuaries were more prevalent than homesteads? And what were the once lives of these parishioners? Where were their habitations? When had they fled? I had caught hearsay that these faiths had once teemed with adherents, but who abided by sooty histories overheard in coffeehouses? Many of our people, that was who.

I overturned a pew and lay beneath it, unwilling to cede an opportunity to sleep indoors. Would that I had had a bedroll on which to lay my unmucked head!

But as I had done before, I awoke to clamor and calamity! Brothers harangued the walls of my shelter, casing the unhallowed church. Their torches scarred shadows inside that loomed above my terrified person like a coven of djinns. From my position beneath a pew, the Brothers seemed again to be atop me. The report of rifles set a roosting owl aflight, and the rattle of the doorway's chains, I thought, would be enough to awaken the dreaming pastor.

I could hear the Brothers outside as they harangued one another and argued about whether to enter or just set the place ablaze. I fingered the page from my aunt's Holy Book and lay as still as a corpse in a garlanded bier, praying that they would not! That they could not! I imagined the Brother with the darkened lenses, flames dancing in his eyes.

My breath left me as the Brothers set their torches on the church. The fire lit the façade and smoke began to crowd the nave, nearly bullying me from my hideout and into their uncharitable embrace!

And my prayer yet again responsed by the Lord!

A timely downpour both quenched the flame and the aspiring intruders! The Lord, as was His wont, sent a deluge! And with it the Brothers' mayhem receded, until I could once again heed the bats.

I remained under the pew or in its vicinity for at least another day.

When finally I readied to quit the sanctuary, such that it was, I saw that a raven nested on the window through which I had entered, and a spider's web thick as clotted milk concealed the shattered pane! I thought it best to undisturb these protecting machinations and pried a rear window open, using a large cross as a makeshift crowbar. I made my way back to the transverse in Pastor Garrett's boots. The Lord be praised.

When the Brothers apprehended me, I had been inhabiting a spider-hole on scabrous former farmland in a valley of the Kansan southwest. On the horizon, the blue rocks stabbed dutifully at the sky. They seemed to defy the laws, such as they are, of the natural world. Would that I had had a chance to savor their luscious snow.

Near the fortified border, I heard the Colorado Guardsmen grind rounds into cannons. The discharge from their munitions wafted to my subterranean hideaway, and with their rifles they burst apart barking rodents. A deadly lot with their aim, and never were my meals so plentiful. Or sulfurous.

Buzzards in great numbers circled low, but in the evenings, I rolled open the skin of sod that secreted my underground cave and hunched to the ground like a picker of a savory and ineffable cotton to retrieve these beheaded squirrels and groundhogs, staining my hands with gore as I tore their bellies with piked fingernails and slurped down their paltry meat and briny livers, which were—I am unashamed to admit—a delicacy to one inured to a diet of pests and berries.

One forenoon as I whittled my claws in the gloom of my hole, the world above me thundered and shook. Rain came by way of dirt. My habitations started collapsing. Did I fear being interred before my time? I did!

Missourians? Miners? Brothers?

No! No! And no!

As the trembling subsided, hooves tore through the sod. The shank of an ungulate dropped into my habitat and flailed and kicked, before the resolute beast sprung himself from my unwitting trap.

And after him, I scampered into the daylight. A pack of camels, the wild horde, galloped across the scrub! They stopped to pick at the remains of rodents before a ball from a Coloradoan's cannon scattered them.

But I had seen them! The untamed camels of the west! Ripe for domestication and husbandry! A new life could be inaugurated by harnessing these beasts!

But while I fantasized about taming camels and riding them across the border, the Brothers explored. They suffered luxuries that in my hunted condition I was not afforded: They travelled by daylight; they were not garbed in clothing ordained for women; they did not rely on rodents for sustenance.

I was kneeling as if in prayer when they breeched my seclusion. Cursed sunlight streamed in, followed by a Brother who pothered up a dust cloud when he landed inside. Other goons fell in behind him.

I wish I could say that from this point, I was luminary.

My blade, gaunt and rusted, rested atop my pack. I shot off the floor, nullifying my prayers, snatched the instrument, and then charged into the nearest Brother, slipping the knife into his flank. The boy cried out, and his mirrored hat toppled as he contorted away from my successful assault.

The Brother behind him squawked, "We bring greetings from your aunt." I recognized him as the oversized one, the pretend lieutenant, who retained the darkened lenses.

I grabbed the bloody blade from the fellow I had stabbed and made slashing motions.

"Death to Bandits!" I shouted.

The bespectacled Brother inquired about the page of my aunt's Holy Book, but I refused to relinquish it.

He then crashed the butt of his rifle into my forehead.

...to Him we shall return.

THE BLACK BIRD

Apparently, my knavery had not gone unnoticed or unannounced. And the way my capture was celebrated, I could have travelled from the Kawsmouth to the South Platte by the light of my own burning effigy!

During my absence from the mosque, the Brothers manufactured a witness who testified to my scheming presence in the coffeehouse on the night of my cousin's passing! Why had he waited so long to divulge the information, I queried? But it did not seem to matter. The suspicious took this fellow at his word, and the testimony, my brief appropriation of my cousin's beads, combined with my disappearance and theft of the page from my aunt's book, as well as whatever the young man in ill-fitting trousers had chronicled, sufficed for enough evidence to condemn me.

Was I given a trial? Was there a qadi in my defense?

There was not!

After being captured by the Brothers in the spider-hole, I have been entombed in my tower. They have cast me off—abandoned me in the minaret to waste away, to raisin up like a goat turd in the sun. I am like Khurram imprisoned in his walled city! Without even the pastor's boots to comfort me!

The Brothers stripped bare my chambers but for a stack of scriptures, my straw mat, and my nightmares. But the powder cask and its foul air remains. Would that I had matches with which to inflame it!

And so, if lives like states have a certain geometry, then mine is not the stalwart square but the suspect circle, incarcerated in what was once my bedroom. Bars have replaced my window, and the doorway has been bricked. With hands devout, I have noticed, it takes no time to accomplish any deed.

In my more vigorous moments, I had thrust my person at the door, but it refused my entreaties. There is for me, it seems, no escape from this place.

Alone I rot with only our stories to sustain me. But with the walls of my tower wilting, I am nearing the end of mine. If I have spoken falsely or have been unforthcoming, may the Lord send a ravenous buzzard to pick at my spleen!

Would only that our stories were as plentiful as the urchins that needed to tell them.

The imam, the Brothers, the Clothed Women, worshippers, migrants, immigrants, pilgrims, Delegates, Partisans, and even Ms. A_____—have all decamped for the Kawsmouth to once again exsanguinate Missourians. For that, I wish them well.

This time, however, their aim is to smooth the only irregular border in our State, to rectangularize Kansas without my assistance, or that of my ascendant cousin, or even of the Brown men. Our State will have a divine, ordained, and rectilinear symmetry. If this be from the Lord, then He will surely bring it to pass. The Lord be praised.

And where is the Black Goat? I suspect that he's slavering behind the front lines. Shall I be cargoed in the bed of his cart? Wrapped in muslin? I shall not, but perhaps there will be a nice pyre!

My hands find my face, and I wave my fingers over my ears as if cooling myself with well-water. Blissful, momentary deceptions are all I have.

To be trapped in this raging room is a torture I wish on no one man.

But perhaps on one woman and several men.

The wind whistles in, carrying the scent of summer bales. It cools me for the moment. Of all the chores mandated to me in the mosque, expiring is the most burdensome. Will I ever find my Garden of Immortality?

Blasts rattle my cage. Missourians not miners. They inspire fissures in the minaret to reveal themselves. Cracks like human spines trace their way from floor to ceiling beside the long bones of my cell's bars.

Knives grate together, blade-on-blade, in flat strokes. Has someone come for me? I envision a chanting stadium. The field is specked with a rust-colored spray. I am one of many in today's bloody parade. My blindfolded frame kneels at the center of a pit. My arms are bound behind me. A bearded man creeps up from behind, barefoot. The plains wind tangles his beard as it does his robe. Darkened lenses shield his eyes. Brackish water floods my mouth. A glinting blade, curved like a scythe, forked like a copperhead's tongue, descends in a frenzied arc.

The crowd's ululation jolts me awake from a heat- and hunger-produced delirium. I prop myself up on my twine-bound pallet. Festooned in stalk, I shake clean. How I wish it were evening when the locusts hiss and the bats… and the bats….

An inky hook scrapes at the bars of my cell. It is a nightmare-inducing bird that had me hallucinating my own beheading! His beak darts between the iron as if playing a tenderfoot's game. His silhouette projects on my wall and rings my head as if I were a bird-prince bedecked by feathered crown.

I ease my feet to the floor and snatch at pale corn kernels, my last meals. A plate of lamb was placed even before Yahudha! The morsels riot my stomach as if they were chevon fresh from slaughter. My pastoral life and all its possible, more intriguing variants rests in this body of corn. Each day as the pile diminishes, I consume the remainder of my life just as I try to sustain it.

The bird gawks at me like I'm an ornithological wonder who hoards his seed rather than join the flock atop the mosque's dome. In bursts, he addresses his avian congregants. Does he tell them of my stash? Or does he keep this undisclosed, just between us. Of those with whom I have shared secrets, this bird will be the last. Oh Lord who is the Avenger of Mankind, deliver me from this place! Safeguard the one who holds Your name!

The murder caws in response to my visitor. Why are crows, so inelegant with their calls, so plentiful in this world? My eyesight fails. I cannot resolve their forms and instead see a windblown sheet. They could abscond with the dome and deliver it someplace far off if they desired. Perhaps to smother elephant-bound riders.

There are many more crows than I can remember, although I haven't glanced outside since the combatants deployed. They took with them that novitiate Brother who served as my warden and house boy, fetching my starchy meals when they were provided—as if the fields of Kansas were not seeded with meat—and replaced my frothing bedpan. The cessation of the former activity has led to the cessation of the latter.

I reach my spidery finger to the obsidian of the crow's beak. With a beat of his wings and a slow swooping drop, he joins his roiling brethren. An inspiring end to this tepid incursion.

"Go West!" sang Maryam's heart and she fled in the night with her Divine son.

My urge: to slip between these bars, sprout wings from my hairy and unblemished shoulders and disappear into the sky, far far from here. I'll leave a lardy mark on the mosque's turban as the others have, and then proceed west, over the flat-lands and the scalloped cuestas and alight in Colorado, where on the cool mountains I will make a new and obscenely better perch. And I will drink drink drink from the Lord's streams that surge through that State like coursing veins.

My fingers find the scar that parts my scalp, delivered by the bespectacled Brother the day I was uncovered. For a time after, my head found itself again bandaged.

"It is a perfect symmetry," my aunt would say, "that the good Lord above does love." Perhaps that's giving those goons too much credit.

Let my clouds be cleared.

Exhale as you say it: *In the name of the Almighty, Gracious and most Merciful Lord.*

The sun pulls taut the tarp of my skin. With its thousand fingers, it peels the paint from the walls so that it droops from the minaret in fleshy strips like the hanging skin of a burn victim.

Heal us! with your touch as you did the cripple child.

My cell convulses as if besieged by a late summer gale. A steady hum, a buzzing follows like the sound of angry hornets! Skins of paint crash down. Beside the bars, the vertebral cracks advance.

Another blast.

Missourians?

And then all is quiet.

What is this, a new chapter in our State?

If there is one thing my solitude has afforded, it is time for reflection. I realize now, as I waste away here, that I was not raised entirely on lies and deception. At least some of what was taught to me was Revelation. That I still ended up in this mausoleum is testament to the failure of those who stewarded my upbringing. Of this I am certain!

Did my aunt even visit me after my capture and incarceration?

No, she did not! But for a while the porridge provided for me was hers—I could never forget its taste.

Did the imam visit me in the tower?

He did, and so I now court more blemishes and welts on my skin than did my cousin on his!

The crow returns. He flits about the ledge. Feathers obscure his oily eyes.

My limbs vestigial from a lack of movement, I stammer like a suckling calf, knocking over a stack of unillustrated Holy Books. In uncertain steps, I am at the iron bars of my cage. I require leg braces once again. For this I should be thankful? My head spins, before settling into me. All this struggle to traverse the once familiar empire of my room.

A blessed breeze whips in, and in an indigo flash the bird flutters inside. To call my guest a crow seems impolite. There is a decorum to naming, this much I know. The curve of the bird's beak suggests an intimate violence. What do you know, Faisal Bird?

And then he is gone.

I am drenched again. Sweat, from terror, from heat, stains the mat, which reeks from my captivity as if I dwell in a fouled barnyard. I take it as a good sign that although I have not had water in many days—as if there were not a perfectly good well in our compound—my skin still sheds its own!

Would that I could reek of rosewater. And who would've thought I'd ever want that?

Heat has made tender the walls, and with a fingernail I carve a glyph of a woman into the minaret. She is a crude rendering, and my hands ache.

You may think that I have been too hard, my judgments needlessly, perhaps viciously, unfavorable to womenkind. You would be incorrect. For I must tell you of one final insult, one final betrayal committed by that kind on my person.

And by Ms. A_____ nonetheless!

While I wandered our storied plains, fleeing the Brothers, my love—a term that I use loosely—with the assistance of a Talib and my aunt gave birth to my son. I was correct, of course, for I knew from conception that she would bear a boy. For is He not also the All-Knowing One.

After my capture and imprisonment, Ms. A_____ did bring the infant boy child up the hundred-odd steps of the minaret to visit his father!

The story is as such: I had been tending to the headwound delivered to me by that bespectacled Brother, when I heeded faint footsteps on the stone. That they sounded like my cousin's did not fail to tremble me as I thought that maybe he'd been made a djinn and sought to haunt me. But perhaps that was my seclusion merrymaking with my sentiments.

Then, there came a loud rapping on the slab door, which had been only partially bricked up at the time. The noise was like a thunder, and so when I slid the port open and saw Ms. A_____, I assure you I was shook that she could elicit such a racket!

For the first and last time, I met Ms. A_____'s gaze with my own. Her face was afire with hostile certainties! Nearly everything I had admired about her sunken and placid demeanor seemed replaced by a fury—as if a whirlwind had possessed the form of a lady!

Though she was afire, she knew her visit was a breach of decorum, for she kept sneaking looks down the stairs in case anyone might find her and hastily return her to safety.

"The child," she whispered. "I need you to know a thing about him." Despite the fury on her face, her deliverance was steady as if rehearsed for so many nights in the very coffee-house she had tended. I will tell you that there is no more fearsome a tongue than that of a woman who has practiced the lesson she is about to convey.

Ms. A_____ held the infant to the slit in the doorway where I, for the last and first time, witnessed my son. He was small, smaller than I thought a boy should be. As if born not into a world that would rid itself of infidels, but one that was overrun by them!

That the boy did not mewl, I was saddened by. I would've liked to hear him so that I could remember him now.

His face though—it bore a resemblance to his father's, with tufts of black hair and hollowed-out cheeks. His eyes and nose: alert, prominent, defiant, unbloodied. Ordained for a great purpose! Although not remembering fully what my own face looked like was not a help.

I shoved a hand through the opening to stroke his face, but before I could touch him, Ms. A_____ pulled the child away and wrapped him across her back.

"The naming ceremony," she continued in her fearsome, steadfast manner. "We will have that and then decamp."

And before I could ask, she answered with: "His name will be Faisal. The boy's name will be Faisal. Faisal bin Faisal. After his father."

And with that, Ms. A_____ slammed shut the slab door on my hand, occasioning contusions! And then the only sound I heard was that of her fading footsteps as she descended the tower, taking my child with her!

A pain tore into me like a hawk at my liver.

A pain tore into me like a limb severed by a hatchet.

A pain tore into me like a deer disassembled by a land torpedo.

A pain tore into me like calloused hands at my throat.

Just as I never knew one could weep in happiness until the

day I learned I was to be a father, I never knew that pain could be delivered in so many forms on a person—and all at once! I am certain it was no less the feeling than when the Prophet was forced to flee B_____ for Y_____.

I am not ashamed to admit that I had to wipe my eyes then.

I wish I could say that after Ms. A_____'s revelation I was afire. That I found the strength to burst through the walls of my familiar cell. That I sequestered my boy from his mother— before he was to be given that woeful name—and on a white horse or a dressed camel galloped into the hinterland.

But there is no truth to any of it. Only fanciful thinking. The product of a desperate imagination that craved a divine and brutal justice.

If you have gotten to this part of the tale, then I need not tell you what effect this pronouncement might have had on my entrapped person. As I have said, I have learned that some-times to gain knowledge is to court dread. Well sometimes, to gain knowledge is also to hold that dread in your bare hands, press it into your body, and let its fever strip you of flesh until you are no more than a headless, limbless, splayed-out hide.

For that was how I felt.

And I resigned myself to that feeling and soon after, to my imprisonment.

And yet I cannot quit her entirely.

Perhaps because I have known no other, I am calling the glyph of the woman I carved into the wall of my tower by her name: Ms. A_____. She is now the placid beauty I had long sought after: Her hair winds around the wall's flourishing fissure. Her chest is modest and tastes piquant to my starved tongue. I replace her areolae in favor of another set of eyes.

They are the color of a quarry lake in my imaginings. How nice it is to have someone watch over you.

I scrawl the word 'bawd' on her thighs. My tattooed lady.

I sniff at the fabric I rescued the night of our consultation, but it no longer holds her scent.

Between hunger and thirst, I have cultivated thirst more. I press my cracked lips, my treasured tongue to the coarse pallet. I cannot extract a drop. Instead, I lap the seep from the withered stalks of my legs, the shallow pools of my shoulders, gnaw each fingertip as if they held Maryam's milk, and relish the salty stingo of the chaff that lodges in my teeth.

The buzzing returns. My teeth rattle, and I spit one out.

F_____'s tongue gave out its shrill call.

I shuffle to the iron bars.

A twist of rope dangles outside the minaret. I slip my arm through the bars, but I cannot reach it.

The strand retracts and pulls away.

The crow returns!

His masked eyes register my presence, although he's keen on my remaining seeds. Vile bird! I coax him to my palm with a kernel. I stroke the dark head. He flitters away. A patch of redness weaves across my right arm. The thistle of ill omen.

If there is a profit to being imprisoned, it is this: Since I was a tenderfoot, I have admired the view from my tower. The grandeur and desolation that distinguishes the Great Plains. A beautiful Country. When worshippers colonized the mosque and the field teemed with pilgrims and immigrants, I could imagine that I was an ancient maharaja surveying my kingdom.

Like a king staring at his citadel. My now dispeopled kingdom.

A blast showers paint. Missourians.

Prairie wolves howl.

They seem frightfully near. But unless they can scale a tower, I have nothing at all to fear from them anymore!

Perhaps for liberating me from this dread, you are to be thanked!

The buzzing is back! Surely the signs are multiplying that my salvation is at hand!

The rope again dangles, and I slam myself against the bars of the windows but find that my frailty cannot liberate them or myself from the minaret. Instead, bruises sprout over my frame. The incision on my forehead gapes. A sanguine syrup stains my beard. I suck out what I can. Once again, my head needs bandaging. I am reverting, regressing.

Oh F_____, how did you know to when to call?

I return to my pallet and scour myself in a manner that can be called feline, yet even cats are not as fastidious as a juiceless man hoarding his juice. If I could piss a stream, I would aim at my mouth. But I am beyond such simple pleasures. It is a winged and feathered meal I require.

Oh F_____, have the Browns ever seen a fighter such as yourself?

The bird arrives! I coax it into my palm with a kernel. The penultimate meal.

I stroke its beak. My fingers clench around its husk. It struggles and fouls. The crow gnaws at the leather of my hand but cannot draw blood. I wrench its neck, and its oily eyes fade. What did you know, Faisal Bird?

And then did a cannonade of stones rain down on them
And crush them so they floundered like fish.

Buzzing again! Wind ruffles the once crow.

Rain comes by way of whitewash.

I dissect the animal with my fingernails and slurp down its organs and its sweet sweet heart. My stomach revolts at the appearance of meat, of sustenance. I sputter black feathers, which list from my mouth to the floor.

I portion the bird over several days.

A quiet strength returns.

The floor of the cell is littered with feathers and brittle paint that cracks beneath my unsure feet.

I will be ready when the buzzing returns.

Oh F_____, how true was your aim, which men did you brain?

The buzzing and the blasts are back!

I would have never praised the Missourians, but for assisting my possible escape from the minaret with their indiscriminate assault, they are thanked!

Crevasses form on the walls, guillotining the glyph of my tattooed love. Where will I find you, Ms. A_____?

A Redeemer in an inflated ark hovers above my tower. Who is he? That too I do not know. A feast of my knowledge would starve a crow.

Again with the buzzing! It's a fat, warship blimp!

In anticipation, I propped the powder keg against the barred window and stacked Holy Books for kindling. Incendiary dust trails to my straw mattress. Unlike my earlier attempt at quitting the mosque, this time I am certain I shall not return!

Goodbye, I say goodbye. The Lord be praised.

With the crow's salvaged beak, I scratch at the ground to provoke sparks. Would that I had my leg braces!

But the buzzing forsakes me before the fire catches!

I am weary for the exertion.

We will join you with the Lord when our time comes.

Oh F_____, save us from that day!

My Savior returns!

I pile straw, pages from the Books, and blast powder into a rat's heap. I scrape the crow's beak against the brittle floor to ignite the kindling. It fails to catch, and the buzzing subsides.

My eyesight had reappeared, but now it seeps from me as if instead of tears, I shed sight.

I refocus on the cracks in the splintering wall. On my back, I flail and kick at the image of my love to cleave apart the bars that imprison me. This project fails. I require tobacco and papers. And a match box. Above all, I need lucifers!

Let my clouds be cleared.

The buzzing recommences, but I have quit the intentions of liberating myself. They too have raisined up in the heat.

What use is this keg if it cannot kindle!

I hurl myself at the barrel and succeed in disengorging powder across the minaret. And like the repercussions from my many, some might say, impetuous actions, a fortuitous and wonderful thing happens: The sunlight colludes with the munition to enflame my pallet!

By the sun and its glorious splendor—the Lord provides!

Swiftly and with an ungraceful fortitude, I hurl the burning bed atop what remains of the powder keg and then tear Holy Books apart for their sweet sweet kindling. Then I hotfoot across the room and cower by the doorway until—not Missourians, not miners, but me!—a blast devastates the circular room!

Have I emerged unscathed?

No, I have not. My head hurts in my head. Where is the gauze? Where is the muslin? Bathe me in camphor! Wounds have launched across my person, and my legs are once more wrecked.

Into this world I entered a cripple, and I shall quit the minaret as one. For this Faisal, you should be thanked!

I crawl across the wrecked house to the window. The glyph of my love has been annihilated, but I find that I can squeeze my scant person through the opening occasioned by the blasting keg. The Lord does love a perfect symmetry.

Hovering above the minaret is the pregnant hull of a warship blimp. These meager mechanisms to manumit those who mourning mothers imprisoned!

This time, unlike when I last left, I know it is the last time. I will float with this balloon far from here. This much I know. Beautiful, bountiful, Colorado! This time, I will be the ascendant one. This time, there will be stones in my mouth and a proper crown on my head.

I step out of the tower and grasp the golden braid that dangles from the dirigible. Not Missourians. Not miners. The reflection of flames dances along the rope.

The sky breaks above me, but I do not shudder, I do not cower.

The crows shriek and circumnavigate the blimp as if it's a vestige from a more resolute time.

The day of calamity is at hand: My habitations are enflamed! Soon too shall the entire minaret be afire. It shall topple and set the mosque ablaze! Then my dispeopled kingdom, the coffeehouse, the well, the outhouses—all will be in ruins! When the Victors return, our State in its final, glorious form, they shall know the name of their Lord.

A slow smirk blooms across my face.

"ad Allah per Aspera!" I cry out and step into the sky.

Oh F_____, when you returned to us unscathed, a hero in your own Land,

Did you know how we loved you?

BLIMPS

I went outside as the sky filled with blimps. To see. Dirigibles of all sizes berthed themselves on any conceivable obelisk— ladders, towers, hillocks, and the minaret, which looked like a child holding a balloon on a string. Airships parked atop airships daisy-chaining their way to the Heavens or the clouds or whatever was over us. They helixed in the air, they spiraled, they dove like rolling pigeons. They looked like they would drop us pamphlets or twists of tobacco, that the sky would open and drown us in things that we hadn't even known we needed but were so thankful for—you couldn't help but wonder how they all knew to come here. Kansas had not seen so many flying things, I am sure, ever. I counted them until they reached the numbers at the edge of my aptitude—as I have said, I am not a scholar. The mass of blimps clotted our limit-less horizon (or so I had so naively thought). More and more kept coming, hovering in the sky like enormous sinking jewels. They squeezed out any traces of what was once above. Then it was dark. And nothing new came. Their growing numbers had stopped. You looked up, where else would you look? And we were sealed inside a giant tube, all surface, no edge, nowhere. Those primitive bugs. Slugs of the sky. Pathetic.

ABOUT THE AUTHOR

Raised in the great state of Kansas, Farooq Ahmed is a graduate of the Columbia University Creative Writing Program and of Brown University, where he studied biochemistry. He is a Contributing Editor for *Photonics* magazine, and his writing has appeared in the *Financial Times*, *Nature*, and the *Proceedings of the National Academy of Sciences*. His work has been lauded by the South Asian Journalists Association, and he lives in Los Angeles. You can find him on Twitter (@farooqtheahmed).

CPSIA information can be obtained
at www.ICGtesting.com
Printed in the USA
LVHW091800250919
632253LV00005B/806/P